THE DISTINCTLY COMPETENT DISTRICT COUNCILLOR

ALSO BY JONAS JONASSON

The Prophet and the Idiot

Sweet Sweet Revenge Ltd.

The Accidental Further Adventures of the Hundred-Year-Old Man

Hitman Anders and the Meaning of It All

The Girl Who Saved the King of Sweden

The Hundred-Year-Old Man Who Climbed Out of the Window and Disappeared

THE DISTINCTLY COMPETENT DISTRICT COUNCILLOR

JONAS JONASSON

Translated from the German
by Ruth Martin

4th ESTATE • London

4th Estate
An imprint of HarperCollins*Publishers*
1 London Bridge Street
London SE1 9GF

www.4thEstate.co.uk

HarperCollins*Publishers*
Macken House, 39/40 Mayor Street Upper
Dublin 1, D01 C9W8, Ireland

First published in Great Britain by Fourth Estate in 2026

1

Copyright © Jonas Jonasson 2026
English translation © Ruth Martin 2026

Jonas Jonasson asserts the moral right to be identified
as the author of this work in accordance with the
Copyright, Designs and Patents Act 1988

A catalogue record for this book is
available from the British Library

ISBN 978-0-00-876737-2

This novel is entirely a work of fiction. The names, characters
and incidents portrayed in it are the work of the author's imagination.
Any resemblance to actual persons, living or dead, events or
localities is entirely coincidental.

All rights reserved. No part of this publication may be
reproduced, stored in a retrieval system, or transmitted,
in any form or by any means, electronic, mechanical,
photocopying, recording or otherwise, without the
prior permission of the publishers.

Without limiting the exclusive rights of any author, contributor
or the publisher of this publication, any unauthorised use of
this publication to train generative artificial intelligence (AI)
technologies is expressly prohibited. HarperCollins also exercise
their rights under Article 4(3) of the Digital Single Market
Directive 2019/790 and expressly reserve this publication
from the text and data mining exception.

Typeset in Sabon LT Std
Printed and bound in the UK using 100%
renewable electricity at CPI Group (UK) Ltd

This book contains FSC™ certified paper and other controlled
sources to ensure responsible forest management.

For more information visit: www.harpercollins.co.uk/green

THE DISTINCTLY COMPETENT DISTRICT COUNCILLOR

DEAR READERS

The times we live in are anything but simple, with war and conflicts everywhere, and it was for this reason that I felt the urge to write something that might give us hope. I wanted to write about friendship between people from different nations. Between my Swedish compatriots, for example, and the Germans, of whom I have grown very fond in recent years. And what came out was this story about a small town in Sweden where things are difficult: unemployment, young people moving away – even the local bookshop has had to close. It doesn't get much worse than that! But when blue and yellow meets black, red and gold, things finally start looking up …

With this in mind, I hope you enjoy my small contribution to German-Swedish friendship. Happy reading!

Warm regards,
Jonas Jonasson

CHAPTER 1

Kaltenbacher and Kaltenbacher

Bloody Scandinavians. Especially the Swedes!

It had taken Konrad Kaltenbacher fifty years to conquer the whole world. All right, nearly the whole world. In Buenos Aires, nobody slept better than the people who got into a Traumbett bed at night. It was the same in Melbourne. Shanghai. Montreal. Tokyo. New York. And in the Johannesburg Sheraton, not to mention the Hilton in Cairo.

Traumbett – because you've earned a good night's sleep.

Sweden, though! Three attempts to crack the market over the years – all with the same crushing result.

Behind closed doors, Konrad was willing to admit the Swedes knew a thing or two about bed manufacturing. But it still vexed him that in these three very wealthy countries – Sweden, Norway and Denmark – hardly anyone slumbered on a Traumbett. It almost kept him up at night.

He was seventy-five now. And a big cheese in Hamburg, if you wanted to put it that way. Universally admired for what he'd achieved. No one would ever guess that he was still so preoccupied by what he *hadn't* achieved.

Well, one person would: Konrad Kaltenbacher Jr, the Bed King's son. Nothing and no one could have made his father prouder. Junior was ready to take over the business now – he had been for some time – and he would do an excellent job!

But the son knew his father. He had tentatively asked permission to mount a final, decisive assault on Scandinavia. This time, they wanted to go 'all in', as the Americans would say. Not just sales and marketing, but a new factory with eight hundred employees. Their existing production capacity in Hamburg needed to be expanded, anyway. And Junior was toying with the idea of investing the money in Oslo, Copenhagen or Stockholm instead.

'Traumbett goes Scandi!' said Konrad Junior in English when he announced his idea.

By now Konrad Senior had made his peace with the fact that these days anyone who had something to say in the field of advertising said it in English. In fifty years, the German language would have died out, you could bet on it. And Swedish, too – well, so be it. At least he'd be dead and buried long before then.

All the same, his son had been doing some very sensible thinking. He'd spent the last three months planning, calculating and analysing. All of it at the mahogany desk in the Traumbett CEO's office.

Six months ago, he had taken over this imposing office and the secretary that went with it, Frau Müller. It sent a signal to the firm's employees: not long now, and Konrad Kaltenbacher would be stepping into the shoes of Konrad Kaltenbacher! However old the old man was, Traumbett would still be as dynamic as ever.

But officially, Konrad Senior remained CEO. Which meant he walked into his son's office without knocking. You had to draw the line somewhere.

'Welcome, Father!' said Konrad Junior, who was already sitting in one of the two leather armchairs in the meeting space. The other was waiting for the head of the company.

Konrad Junior had a pile of papers on his lap. On a little

side table between the chairs, a full glass of mineral water was standing ready for the son, and a glass of cognac for the father.

Konrad Senior took his seat, nodded approvingly at the brandy and came straight to the point: 'So you've made a decision?'

With a smile, his son replied that the CEO still made the decisions around here, but yes, he had come to the conclusion that: 'From a logistical point of view, Oslo isn't in the best location, and the cost of the factory site I've found there is about half our national GDP.'

The son waited respectfully for the father to swallow his first sip of cognac before continuing: 'Copenhagen is the closest to our HQ and the factory here. That has its advantages but also its disadvantages. Sweden is the country we want to crack first and foremost, in which case it seems less than ideal if our Scandinavian branch is closer to Hamburg than to the Swedish capital.'

'And the advantage?'

'Possibly the price.'

A second pause for effect.

'Would you like another sip before I go on?'

Konrad Senior said that could wait. 'Stockholm, then?' he enquired.

The junior boss nodded. 'So far, all I've seen are pictures and approximate figures, but there's a perfect site in Frihamnen, a former container port fifteen minutes from the city centre with excellent transport links. The city council's lead member for finance is super keen, and she doesn't have any preconceived notions that Swedes ought to sleep in Swedish beds.'

'And why should she? Eight hundred new jobs will give her the best chance possible of surviving the next election,' Senior muttered.

'My thoughts exactly,' agreed Junior. 'Having said that, the monthly rent is a hundred and thirty thousand …'

'Krona or euros?'

'Euros, I'm afraid.'

Konrad Senior shrugged. 'Peanuts, if everything else is right. Are you ready to fly out and take a closer look?'

'Yes and no,' the son replied. 'The girls and I are going in the car.'

'You and your car!' said the father.

The son smiled. 'Me and my girls, more like. I find it easier to think when I'm behind the wheel, and with the twins singing in the back, it's even more fun.'

CHAPTER 2

First day in the job

Greater Hamburg was home to a good five million people – and they all knew the name Konrad Kaltenbacher, the city's Bed King.

Halstaholm, a hundred kilometres southwest of Stockholm, was home to eight thousand, two hundred and eight people. And very few of them had heard of Julia Bäck.

Or, to put it more kindly: Halstaholm was of a size where most people vaguely knew one another. But the news that twenty-nine-year-old Julia had just become the mayor of this small, moribund town had only been printed in the local paper, and these days hardly anyone could afford the subscription.

So it was no surprise that the older gentleman out walking his dog threw Julia no more than a cursory glance as she passed him with her briefcase.

'Good morning,' she said, cheerfully.

'It's morning all right,' said the dog owner. 'But I don't see what's good about it.'

One of the many people who had lost their jobs and would sooner or later be claiming an early pension, thought Julia. Ah well, at least he still lived here, unlike so many others. And paid his dog tax, with any luck. Every little helped!

The newly minted mayor carried on along the main road, past the town's only row of shops. Half were shut because it was still early. The other half were shut for good: Halsta Sound & Vision, Halsta Books, Wanja's Health Foods ...

Julia wondered for a moment where Wanja had gone after closing up her shop for the last time. Stockholm, most likely, same as all the others.

Her destination was the town hall – which was a bit of a joke, incidentally, just like everything else. Harriet Ljungberg the receptionist – who doubled as a general odd-job woman – was the only person who still had a job there. Except of course the mayor herself. Plus the amateur politicians of the district council, which met once a month. Twenty-one members: eighteen jaded, lacklustre characters, a senile ninety-year-old (no one could remember how she had gained her seat at the table, or why she was still in it), and the inevitable troublemaker who did nothing but moan and demand the impossible. And now, at the head of the table, Julia Bäck, holding the chair's gavel.

On her first day in the job, the new mayor had to let herself in. Super-Harriet wasn't here yet. And why would she be, when the working day didn't start for another hour?

Julia walked past reception, through the glass doors, and took the stairs to the first floor. As she was heading for her empty desk, the sign on the office door caught her eye:

TORSTEN BLOMQUIST
MAYOR

Her fellow party member Torsten could now devote himself to angling full-time. Thinking about him made Julia smile. He'd been so committed to the good of the district, for twenty-five long years. The first ten had been one victory after another. The town had grown, people moved in, everyone believed in the future.

Until the first signs that the tyre factory was in trouble. Halstadäck had competitors coming out of its ears. Michelin, Goodyear, Nokian ...

Realising how serious the situation was, Torsten had thrown all his weight behind a proposal for the council to borrow a huge sum of money. All seventy-two thousand square metres of the factory were upgraded to become state-of-the-art, in an effort to help the company haul itself out of the crisis.

But it was too late.

That was eleven years ago now. Five hundred and fifty Halstaholmers had been sacked without warning, and Torsten and the town were left sitting on one of the largest and most modern manufacturing facilities in Sweden. Empty as a nest box in December.

While the removal lorries took the road out of Halstaholm instead of going the right way, Julia's predecessor tried to find a new tenant. A hundred thousand krona per month in rent would do it. Or fifty. Or twenty-five.

During Torsten's final two years in the mayor's seat, where Julia had just sat down, the price had sunk to one krona a month. That was just ten euro cents for any international player who was prepared to consider it.

And one had actually shown some interest! An Estonian firm offered to pay the ten cents a month for the six months it would take them to pull the factory down and sell the bricks on the second-hand market for five hundred euros per cubic metre. That was the first and only time Julia heard Torsten swear.

'Sod off back to Tallinn, you cut-throat bastards!' he had exclaimed.

The cut-throat bastards had done just that, and since then there had been nothing new under the sun. Or under the rainclouds. Because it was October already.

Nothing new, not even in the town's unemployment figures, which remained stubbornly at thirty per cent. And the only reason they hadn't risen higher was that so many people were moving away.

To bloody Stockholm, of course. An hour and a half by bus, with a change at Södertälje. In the tyre factory's time, there had been four direct services a day.

* * *

Julia Bäck opened the laptop she had brought with her, connected the cable and started googling. It was as clear as day: bringing the factory back to life was the only alternative to Halstaholm's slow but steady progress towards its own demise.

But that was as far as she got: the office door flew open, and in came Harriet, the general odd-job woman, with a tray of coffee and cinnamon buns and a solitary rose in a small vase. She was also carrying a metal nameplate.

'Good morning, Madam Mayor!' Harriet called out. 'Here I am, with coffee!'

Harriet and Julia had known each other a long time and were on first-name terms, so Julia was fairly sure the 'Madam Mayor' was just in honour of her first day.

The receptionist placed the vase with its rose on the desk in front of Julia.

'This here is from a secret admirer – me, in other words,' she announced.

'Well, I'd have been very surprised if it was anyone else,' said Julia. 'Sadly, the dating scene around here is as bleak as everything else. Which is why I'm staying single – to the end of my days, in all probability.'

Harriet took the aluminium nameplate over to the office door and swapped *Torsten Blomquist Mayor* for *Julia Bäck*

Mayor, then, with the words, 'Sorry, Torsten', threw the old sign in the wastepaper basket in the corner. She set out cups and plates on the round table, also in the corner with two accompanying chairs.

'Come and sit, Julia,' she said. 'The coffee is freshly brewed and the cinnamon buns are from Algot's. By some miracle, they haven't closed down yet!'

Julia thanked her for the rose, and went to join her assistant at the table. The bloom reminded Harriet: 'There are more flowers downstairs at reception. They arrived at the same time I did. I've put them all in water.'

'Are there that many people wanting to congratulate me?'

'Well … depends how you look at it,' mumbled Harriet, through a mouthful of bun. 'Torsten, obviously. Isn't he sweet! And Andersson from Andersson Plumbing – I think he's fishing for work, in case we decide to renovate and reopen the swimming pool. And one more—'

'The swimming pool?' Julia interjected. 'Why would we? So that all the people who haven't moved away yet have somewhere they can drown themselves?'

Harriet's mouth was too full to answer. And Julia seemed to be absorbed in her own thoughts. Silence descended for a while, before the receptionist asked, 'Are you thinking about the factory?'

Julia nodded.

'It's been eleven years since they gave up. Until then I'd been convinced that Halstaholm was heaven on earth … I was eighteen. There were sixteen thousand of us here back then. And now there's eight thousand, two hundred and eight.'

'Soon to be eight thousand, two hundred and four,' said Harriet. 'Yesterday the garden centre man told me he and his family are packing up and most likely moving to Gothenburg. He said he does understand why people don't want to spent the last of their money on rhododendron bushes, but if he can't even sell geraniums now for nine krona each, he doesn't know what else to do.'

'Goddammit!' said Julia. 'This town is sitting on the most modern factory building in the world, and it's just lying there, empty! Did you know it's costing sixty thousand a month just to maintain the sodding thing?'

'For what, exactly?'

'Bloody hell, how should I know? Power, water, heating ... All I've seen are the figures.'

'Wow, you've sworn more in your first half-hour in the job than Torsten did in twenty-five years,' said Harriet, sounding impressed. 'What if you just had the whole thing pulled down? Or could you turn the factory into housing?'

'Housing? People are moving out, Harriet. Not in.'

'I was just thinking ...'

'Excellent! That's exactly what we need! We have to think! As aggressively as we can!'

'Get back into the tyre business?'

'I'm a mayor, not a tyre manufacturer. There must be another option.'

'But what?'

'I don't know. Seventy-two thousand square metres! All still state-of-the-art! I'll flog the lot in a heartbeat for absolute peanuts to anyone who promises to move in and employ people.'

'And pay the electricity bill?'

'Obviously.'

'Who might that be?'

Julia Bäck couldn't answer that.

CHAPTER 3

The mayor and the nameless fish

A mayor who was temporarily at a complete loss finished her first day in the job on her living-room sofa – jogging trousers on, a glass of red wine on the side table, laptop on her lap – while her pet, a guppy, swam solitary lengths in a little aquarium on a shelf.

Julia googled firms who might conceivably be prepared to set up in Halstaholm.

'Speaking of Google, fish,' she said to the nameless guppy, 'how about a Scandinavian base for Google here? But then, do they actually employ anyone over the age of nineteen? And what are five hundred nineteen-year-olds going to do after work in Halstaholm? There are maybe twenty seats in the pizzeria, tops. And not even a pinball machine, or table football.'

The guppy didn't reply.

Julia kept googling.

'IKEA?' she wondered. 'Though we might not have quite the customer base they need – what do you think? Every single person in Halstaholm would probably have to buy a new BILLY bookcase every day. And when you consider that they can't even afford geraniums at nine krona each …'

The guppy remained as silent as before.

Julia continued her search. A headline in the national *Dagens Nyheter* newspaper caught her eye:

IS GERMAN CORPORATE GIANT COMING TO STOCKHOLM?

The German multi-billion company Traumbett is looking for a location in Scandinavia. Reliable sources say that an urban industrial site in Frihamnen is streets ahead of competition from Oslo and Copenhagen. A Traumbett factory could generate hundreds of new jobs for the Swedish capital. And it would be the largest branch of a German company to be established in Sweden since ...

Julia skimmed the rest.

Manufacturing, distribution, sales ...

She turned to the guppy in the tank. 'What do you reckon, fish? Should we bet on the Germans, and make Halstaholm the bed capital of Scandinavia?'

The mayor, who had been slumped on the sofa, sat bolt upright and struck a ceremonial tone: 'Welcome to Halstaholm, the dormitory town.'

As if a snappy slogan could solve anything.

'Move to Halstaholm: a good night's sleep guaranteed!'

Still no word from the guppy.

'I miss your encouragement, fish. Are you angry with me for not giving you a name yet?'

The evening was getting late – time for some shut-eye in her own IKEA bed. Julia Bäck had made a decision. Tomorrow, she was going to call Hamburg. The new mayor got up from the sofa and switched off the aquarium light with a final word to her only companion: 'If this works out, you'll have to learn to not talk in German as well.'

CHAPTER 4

A call from the White House

Konrad Kaltenbacher Jr was sitting at his mahogany desk with three dossiers in front of him: Stockholm, Oslo, Copenhagen. He felt he needed to mull over the options one last time, without any distractions. The heir to the firm had just convinced his father to stay in the top job for at least another few years. Then Konrad Junior and his girls could move to – well, would it be Stockholm, now? – and personally make sure that the last white spot on the Traumbett map was coloured in.

But the choice would have far-reaching implications. He spoke to his secretary through the intercom: 'Frau Müller ... good morning. Would you please hold all my calls until lunchtime? I have some thinking to do, and I need complete peace and quiet.'

'Yes, of course, Doctor Kaltenbacher,' said Frau Müller.

* * *

Meanwhile, in her rather more humble council office in Halstaholm, Julia Bäck had found the number for the Hamburg bed company and the name of its chief executive. And now she had a German voice in her ear saying, 'Welcome to Traumbett. How can we help you today?'

Julia apologised for replying in English and said that she would like to speak to Dr Kaltenbacher.

'The younger or the older Doctor Kaltenbacher?' the voice asked in English.

What kind of a question was that? How many Kaltenbachers did this firm have? Though maybe the younger one would be more open to new ideas?

'The younger, please.'

'Certainly. But I'm afraid Doctor Kaltenbacher's secretary is extremely busy; can I ask what your call is about?'

Why did they make things so complicated?

'I'm sorry to hear Doctor Kaltenbacher's secretary is so busy, but I don't actually want to speak to his secretary, I want to speak to Doctor Kaltenbacher.'

The receptionist was temporarily lost for words.

'As ... I said,' she replied after a brief pause.

Julia glanced back at her screen, and the article on the *Dagens Nyheter* site announcing that Traumbett might be setting up in Stockholm. And at the browser window open beside it, showing a very different article about tensions between Taiwan and the Chinese mainland. And the concern that US Secretary of State Antony Blinken had expressed about the situation.

Without giving it too much thought, she clutched at this straw and shot from the hip. Putting on the most American accent she could muster, she said: 'Listen, I'm calling from the White House in Washington DC, on behalf of Secretary of State Blinken. It's about sixty-five thousand beds. Or, as the Secretary of State likes to say: *You can't be a good NATO soldier without a good night's sleep.*'

The receptionist fell silent again.

'So would you kindly to put me through to Doctor Kaltenbacher's extremely busy secretary so that I can ask the good lady how busy Doctor Kaltenbacher himself is, because the Secretary of State would like to talk to him?'

'One moment, please,' said the receptionist hastily, before putting Julia Bäck on hold.

* * *

With a deep sigh, Konrad Kaltenbacher took Oslo and Copenhagen and consigned them to the wastepaper bin. It would be Stockholm, plain and simple.

There was a knock on the door, and his secretary walked in without waiting for a response.

'Frau Müller ... wasn't I clear enough about not wanting to be disturbed?' he asked in surprise. Because Konrad Kaltenbacher Jr really was a nice man.

The secretary shifted nervously from one foot to the other. 'I know, Herr Doctor, but there's a call from the White House in Washington. Secretary of State Antony Blinken wants to speak to you.'

'Well, blow me down,' said Konrad Kaltenbacher, straightening up in his executive chair. 'Now? It's the middle of the night in Washington. Right ... well, you'd better put him through.'

The relieved Frau Müller nodded, went out, and put the waiting caller through. When the red light flashed, Konrad Kaltenbacher pressed the speakerphone button and answered in fluent English: 'Doctor Kaltenbacher here. Is this the White House?'

Julia had done it. Desperation really is the mother of invention, and the truly inventive mayor had finagled her way through to the boss of Traumbett. She hoped she had the right boss on the phone. 'Doctor' made him sound like a boss, even if 'the younger' might mean he wasn't the top boss. Now what was she supposed to say?

She hadn't thought that far ahead.

'The White House? No, that must be a misunderstanding. I'm calling to *offer* you a white house! Though in actual fact, it isn't white, it's more of a reddish colour. Anyway, it's exactly what you're looking for, Herr Kaltenbacher, in every way. And it's basically free!'

Konrad Kaltenbacher's suspicion that someone had fibbed their way past his secretary was confirmed. He leaned back in his chair. This conversation wouldn't take long.

'Frau Müller doesn't usually fall prey to misunderstandings.'

'It's a fantastic factory, and pretty much gratis, did I mention that?'

Something – he wasn't sure what – coaxed a little smile from Konrad Kaltenbacher. This woman might be utterly brazen, but there was something creative about her approach. He decided to prolong the conversation a tiny bit. 'Just out of curiosity, may I ask where this almost-gratis red building might be?'

Spurred on by the fact that the doctor hadn't hung up yet, Julia Bäck almost yelled in response: 'In wonderful, wonderful Halstaholm! The Swedish town of the future!'

One corner of Konrad Kaltenbacher's mouth turned up in amusement.

'Sweden? Hmm, well, it's definitely in the right ballpark. And might I know with whom I have the pleasure of speaking?'

This was going really well. Julia was so excited, she hadn't even remembered to introduce herself.

'My name is Julia Bäck, and I'm the mayor and head of the district council in that very town. I'm calling to make you an offer you can't refuse.'

On that point, Konrad Kaltenbacher begged to differ.

'As Traumbett's deputy CEO, I am responsible for the company's Scandinavian strategy. And as such, I can in fact refuse *any* of your suggestions, Mrs Bäck.'

It was just a few months since Julia had kicked her boyfriend out, with good reason, and been left with only the guppy for company.

'It's Miss Bäck,' she corrected him. 'Not Mrs. But speaking of names and titles ... are there *two* Konrad Kaltenbachers in your company? Doesn't that make things tricky for you?'

Now the other corner of Konrad Kaltenbacher's mouth turned up. No doubt about it, the conwoman on the other end of the line was charming.

'Konrad Kaltenbacher Senior is my father; I'm Konrad Kaltenbacher Junior. And unlike you, *Miss* Bäck, we are exactly who we say we are.'

Julia sensed that, despite everything, the German was warming to her.

'Look, let's not quibble about this, Herr Doctor. If I'd said my real name, you would never have taken the call, would you?'

'You could have asked my secretary to get me to call you back.'

'Would you have?'

'No.'

'There you are, then,' said Julia Bäck. 'Now I feel like there's only one question left to ask.'

'Which is?'

'When can you drop by? Seventy-two thousand square metres of space, everything is basically new, in principle all the staff you need are already here, and best of all: you won't have to set foot in Stockholm, Herr Doctor Kaltenbacher! Halstaholm has *everything* you might need!'

'Everything?' the doctor exclaimed.

'Apart from a functioning swimming pool,' Julia admitted.

Konrad Kaltenbacher wasn't sure if this was some kind of phone prank, but he was still finding it entertaining.

'Now listen, Miss Bäck. I should have hung up long ago. Calling this office, claiming to be from the White House – it's utterly shameless!'

But then he was interrupted.

'I want one euro for the whole thing.'

Konrad Kaltenbacher had spent the morning worrying about the 130,000 euros a month in rent for the Frihamnen factory.

'One euro?'

'See, now you get it!' said Julia Bäck. 'You can have the swankiest factory in the world for a euro! And if you have any cashflow issues, we can always agree an instalment plan. All I'm asking is that you set up a branch here in Halstaholm, the town all roads lead to!'

'I thought that was Rome?' Konrad Kaltenbacher shot back.

'Rome and Halstaholm, that's what they say.'

Traumbett made considerable profits in at least 165 countries; revenue far in excess of the one euro Julia Bäck had just asked for.

'May I enquire as to where this Halsta … place is?'

'Halstaholm! A stone's throw southwest of Stockholm.'

'And how far does the average Swede throw a stone?'

Now that was a sore point. Before all the trouble started, it would have been less than an hour by bus, but now you had to change in Södertälje. And Arlanda Airport was another half-hour north of the capital.

'Currently, things could be easier,' Julia conceded. 'But the southern main line is being extended, and two years from now the journey time to the capital will be only twenty minutes.'

Admittedly, that wasn't completely true. There were two potential new main line routes on the table, and the government hadn't decided which to go for yet. But the Halstaholm route was 'Option one', and Julia would have to make do with that for the time being.

Kaltenbacher seemed to be considering what she'd said, so she seized the moment: 'Right, then, when shall we say?' She pretended to consult her diary. 'Hmm, let's see ... next Monday might work.'

No response.

'Ah, or Tuesday, I see now.'

Still nothing. Julia couldn't see or even guess at Konrad Kaltenbacher's growing enjoyment of the whole situation.

'Or Wednesday ... if I move a meeting. Actually, now I'm looking at it, any time that week would be okay.'

'Miss Bäck,' said Konrad Kaltenbacher.

'Yes, Herr Doctor?'

'Seventy-two thousand square metres for one euro sounds acceptable, especially when one considers that you are offering a generous instalment plan. But Traumbett requires a lot of space outside the production facilities, some of it for sales and marketing, some for loading and unloading. But most importantly, we'd need two hundred parking spaces. Is that something Halstaholm can offer?'

Quick as a flash, and wholly untruthfully, Julia said: 'Of course, Herr Doctor Kaltenbacher! Will two hundred be enough? You wouldn't rather have three hundred?'

He couldn't help it. This peculiar person on the phone gave Konrad a good feeling. He was surprised to hear himself saying, 'All right then, Miss Bäck, here's what we'll do: I have a meeting in Stockholm next Wednesday. I'll be driving there with my family. Out of sheer curiosity, we can take a detour to Halstaholm on the way back – let's say at around three in the afternoon on Thursday. Will that fit into your busy schedule?'

Julia pretended to flick through her non-existent diary. 'Let me see. Yes, Thursday just happens to be particularly good.'

'That's settled, then. I'll inform my secretary, and you can agree the details with her tomorrow, okay?'

Julia leaped to her feet in delight and threw both arms in the air as if she'd just scored a goal in a World Cup final.

Konrad Kaltenbacher went on: 'And when you call Frau Müller tomorrow, I don't want to hear that Antony Blinken, Mother Teresa or Nelson Mandela is asking for me. You give her your real name, are we agreed on that?'

'The last two are dead anyway, aren't they?' said Julia.

'I think you understand what I'm getting at, *Miss* Bäck.'

'Yes, Herr Doctor Kaltenbacher. Understood.'

* * *

During the last part of the call, Harriet had walked into the mayor's office. And since Julia had also been on speakerphone, her employee had been able to hear everything.

'The German bed manufacturer?' she said, after Julia had hung up.

'Yes, my dear Harriet – the deal is as good as done!'

The receptionist took a rather more cautious view of the matter. 'How many parking spots *are* there outside the factory? Thirty?' she asked tentatively.

'More like twenty, I'd say.'

'And you just went and promised him two hundred? And offered another hundred if this Herr Whatsisname wanted them?'

'I'll have to give that detail some thought,' said Julia. 'His name's Kaltenbacher, by the way. And apparently the company has more than one of them.'

'And you do know that the government hasn't decided where the new train line is going yet?'

'We're option one, Harriet. Do stop taking such a gloomy view of everything.'

The word 'gloomy' reminded the receptionist that the council's troublemaker-in-chief Hasse Eriksson was waiting downstairs. Harriet could not be doing with him at all.

'Hasse? What does he want?'

'An endless discussion about the swimming pool would be my bet. He's got it into his head that the town would come alive again if only its residents could jump in the water now and then. He's intending to put forward a motion about it at the next council meeting; he wants nine hundred thousand for new pipes, tiles, and all sorts.'

Julia sighed. 'So we need to spend nine hundred thousand of the money we don't have to make the indoor pool fit for use by the residents we also won't have for much longer?'

'Something like that, yes.'

'Go and tell him the mayor is on an important phone call with the US Secretary of State, but he's welcome to make an appointment.'

'I'm not as good at lying as you are, Julia. But when do you think you'll have time for him? Some point next week?'

Julia Bäck pretended to consult her diary again, which until a few minutes earlier had been completely empty – and which still didn't exist.

'Looks like I'm fully booked next week. The week after?'

CHAPTER 5

The member for finance and the management consultant

Ingela Franzén, Stockholm City Council's lead member for finance, could not manage without her freelance adviser Kenneth Carlander. Unfortunately, she didn't manage that well with him, either. It was hard to imagine anyone more irritating. In confined spaces, he could only be endured with great difficulty.

Four hours previously, the German bed businessman had called her back to say that he was satisfied with Carlander's presentation and wanted to drop in for a proper look at the site. But only now, four hours later, had the management consultant seen fit to waltz into the city official's office.

'Morning, sweetie!' said Kenneth Carlander.

'*Mrs Franzén* would be a more appropriate form of address,' the official snapped.

But the consultant was already busy rummaging in her cupboard. 'Don't you have a bottle of whisky in here somewhere? Ah, here it is! No ice? Well, this'll have to do. Want one?'

'Just sit down and listen, you terrible, useless man,' said Ingela Franzén.

Carlander plumped into the chair opposite her, placed a glass of whisky on her desk and took a vigorous gulp from his own.

'More news from the German?' he said. 'That was such an incredible coup I pulled off, getting rid of the last lot. Losers! Sixty squash courts versus eight hundred new jobs for your Stockholm – well, there's only one winner there, hmm?'

Ingela Franzén squirmed. She wasn't sure forcing out the previous tenants had been completely above board, but luckily the management consultant had taken care of it, so it couldn't come back to bite her.

'*The German* has a name: Doctor Konrad Kaltenbacher Junior. And yes, he's been in touch. It seems you've taken Oslo and Copenhagen out of the running. He's coming to Stockholm on Tuesday evening and wants to be shown around the site on Wednesday morning. We'll meet in my office. Can you promise to be here on time and, more importantly, sober?'

'I knew it!' Carlander crowed. 'I'm the *man*! No worries, sweetie, I'll turn up sober. Aren't you going to drink that whisky?'

Without waiting for an answer, he grabbed the glass and chased his own down with it.

Ingela Franzén knew that she could never have attracted Traumbett to Stockholm without the boorish man sitting in front of her. All the same, she longed to be able to throw him out the window. They were on the third floor; that would do it, surely?

'However, there are a couple of problems,' said the member for finance.

'Problems are my speciality,' replied the management consultant, leaning even further back in his armchair – before adding in English, 'Just hand them over.'

Like Konrad Kaltenbacher Senior, Ingela Franzén was of the generation that couldn't understand why people felt the need to switch to English every other sentence.

'You can speak English to the German on Wednesday, if your schoolboy German isn't up to the task. Here and now, kindly stick to Swedish – or better still, just listen.'

She explained that Herr Dr Kaltenbacher had emailed questions to which he wanted answers, such as what was included in the rent, and what options existed for remodelling and extending. But the main thing was the costs for power, water, maintenance and so on.

'No problem, don't you worry about that,' said the consultant.

'Well, it *will* be a problem if you don't have some answers for him by Wednesday!'

'Take it easy,' said Carlander, getting up to move discreetly in the direction of the drinks cabinet.

'Hands off the whisky!' said the member for finance. 'Plus, Doctor Kaltenbacher told me he's planning a detour to Halstaholm on his way back to Hamburg, as a potential alternative to Frihamnen.'

That did distract the consultant from his whisky expedition.

'Shit – what? Halstaholm? Where's that? The arse end of nowhere? What do they have to offer apart from fields and meadows?'

'Fields, meadows – and an old tyre factory,' Franzén explained.

Halstadäck! The word shot through the management consultant's skull. Didn't they close down a decade ago? Well, if they went bankrupt once, he was sure it could be arranged again if necessary.

'If these are your only problems, Mrs Franzén, may I possibly be excused? Kenneth Carlander has heard and understood. Now, I have an important business meeting in town.'

The consultant prepared to decamp.

'Oh yes? Which pub is it in?' Ingela Franzén asked, somewhat coolly. 'And take the questions about electricity, water and so on with you.'

She handed him the pages that Herr Dr Kaltenbacher had emailed her.

'German thoroughness,' sighed the consultant. 'That's all we need.'

'Eight hundred Swedish jobs, you idiot!' said the official.

CHAPTER 6

The mayor's taskforce

Konrad Kaltenbacher Jr loved his black Audi A9 with its tinted windows. Twelve hours from Hamburg to Stockholm, with a few McDonald's breaks along the way.

Good music coming from the speakers and cheerful chatter with the twins in the back seat. Maren and Marie weren't just enchanting, they were his whole world.

He also had plenty of thinking time, when the girls were keeping themselves occupied. Short-term, long-term. Practical. Technical. Strategic. Making secure plans. There was nowhere else he could think as clearly as behind the wheel.

However, he was already regretting having allowed this Julia Bäck in Halstaholm to sweet-talk him. She clearly had a screw loose, and now they wouldn't be back in Hamburg before Thursday night. And the girls had school on Friday.

Still, a promise was a promise. He could probably discount this fairy-tale village in twenty minutes. But one thing at a time. First, they had a long day tomorrow with an early start. Leaving at eight, and checking in to the Grand Hôtel Stockholm at around eight that evening. A quick visit to the gym, so the girls could splash around in the pool, a shower, and dinner. And he could hit the hay at eleven.

* * *

While the German junior boss could think best behind the wheel, Julia Bäck did her best thinking on foot, in the fifteen-minute walk from her little house on the outskirts of Halstaholm to the town hall.

She certainly needed to think – and quickly. It was already Monday, after a deathly boring training course – in Stockholm of all places. Its title had been *The Role of Natural Resources in a Rural Context when Geographical Conditions are Deteriorating*. In three days of jabbering from a British professor, Julia had learned two things: 1) The air was fresher in the countryside than in the city; and 2) Going on a training course was assuredly not the best way to save Halstaholm.

Her route to work took her past the disused tyre factory, among other things. Which enabled the mayor to do a more accurate count of the parking spaces. She made it twenty-two, which could probably be extended to twenty-five if they replaced a few bike racks.

How many had she promised, again? Two hundred? Three hundred? Plus space for loading and unloading. That was another few thousand square metres.

The stream gurgled along behind the factory – it would be hard to fill it in. Julia might not be an expert in watercourses, but she knew that wasn't a good idea.

To the east, the site bordered the town's park. Apathetic as most of the council members were, they were sure to vote down any application to flatten and tarmac over the green space. To say nothing of her best buddy, the troublemaker Hasse Eriksson.

The western, northwestern and northern sides of the factory were the only options. And all that land belonged to old Bolmgren. To make matters worse, he actually *lived* there, in a red log cabin up on the hill. The place wasn't especially attractive to anyone but him, yet he had been there his whole life.

'I need to get Börje Bolmgren on my side,' Julia said to herself, before continuing through the park. 'And I need help!'

She would have to offer Herr Dr Kaltenbacher so much more. The industrial site was the main thing: hers in Halstaholm versus the one in Stockholm-Frihamnen. And Julia knew her offer would bear comparison. The price was right, for one thing.

Everything else would just be a beauty contest. If Julia had understood the secretary in Hamburg correctly, Traumbett's deputy boss wanted to bring his family to Sweden, to move there. Where would he prefer to live? Anyone who had seen a bleak Halstaholm in late October might have difficulty finding the correct answer.

So Julia needed two things before the Kaltenbachers arrived: the first was a miracle; well, those things happened now and then. The other was a taskforce. She would never manage to pull it all together by herself. And the guppy at home was no great help, either.

Halfway across the park, pondering the subject of miracles, she had the misfortune to be addressed by a lone man who was playing boules by himself.

'Good morning, Madam Mayor. Fancy a quick game?'

He appeared to recognise her. True, *Halsta Nytt* had printed an article about her a few days previously, but it still surprised her that the local paper had any readers left.

'Morning,' Julia replied. 'That would be lovely, but I'm afraid I don't have time.'

'That's a shame,' he said. 'I have nothing *but* time.'

Oh dear. She should have known. An unaccompanied, middle-aged, mid-morning boules player. He must have been washed up here by the tidal wave of the factory's bankruptcy.

'Unemployed?' she asked.

'For exactly eleven years now,' the man confirmed.

'Go on, then. There's always time for a game of boules,' said Julia, reaching for the ball the man was holding. She stepped onto the court, spotted the small red jack, aimed – and missed it by several metres.

'I hope you're better at saving towns than you are at throwing balls,' said the boules player.

'Only time will tell,' said Julia. 'I'm trying to bring the tyre factory back to life.'

She immediately regretted letting that slip. After all, the German might take one look at the place and leave. She must not blab too much before he got here – it was no good raising false hopes then being left red-faced and empty-handed.

'Superb!' said the boules player, giving her his hand. 'Bosse,' he added.

'Julia,' said Julia.

'I know,' Bosse replied. 'About the factory ... I worked there for eight years, in quality assurance. Do you think that job might be available again?'

Having said too much already, the mayor decided she might as well keep going.

'Well, it will be German beds this time, not tyres.'

'Traumbett!' said Bosse.

'You read the newspaper.'

'Aren't they going to Frihamnen in Stockholm?'

'Or to Halstaholm,' said Julia.

'Beds have to be quality assured too, wouldn't you say?'

Unemployed and thwarted ... and yet suddenly he was fizzing with energy.

Julia nodded and said it certainly sounded like comfortable work. She had an idea. 'Might you be interested in joining my taskforce?'

Bosse's eyes lit up. 'I'd love to!' he said. 'Who else is on it?'

'Just you and me, so far. And it's a voluntary position.'

He tossed the last two balls randomly onto the court. Both landed in better positions than the one the mayor had aimed.

'Come on then, let's go,' he said. 'Sounds like there's no time to lose. When is the German going to make his decision?'

Julia and Bosse carried on walking side by side. The mayor was about to start telling him about Traumbett's Swedish excursion when a high, despairing voice called out from the top of the tyre pile that Halstadäck had donated as a children's climbing frame.

'Hello, down there in the valley! The air is thin up here, it's hard to breathe, and it's twenty-nine degrees below zero! Do you happen to have any oxygen?'

Julia turned to Bosse. 'I think someone's trying to make friends.' Then to the mountaineer: 'It is rather a foolish move to have climbed Mount Everest without any oxygen! Why aren't you at school?'

The boy hopped quickly and deftly down the pile of tyres.

'It's the last day of half-term. I've never been so bored in my life.'

Bosse said he had been feeling exactly the same until very recently. 'And now I'm the quality assurer on the town taskforce. We're going to get the tyre factory up and running again.'

'The one that closed down when I was still in my mum's tummy?' said the boy.

'Except we want to give high-quality German beds a go, instead of tyres,' Bosse went on.

'Which is something we don't need to tell the *whole* town before the Germans have even had a look at it,' said Julia.

'*Aber wenn Sie die Deutschen für sich gewinnen wollen, können Sie mich vielleicht brauchen?*' the boy responded in fluent German.

'What did he just say?' asked Bosse.

'I have no idea,' said the mayor, turning to the boy again. 'How old are you?'

'Ten.'

'Really? You don't look a day over nine and a half. And what's your name?'

'Peter.'

'Despite your age, your language skills qualify you for my taskforce. Interested?'

'Am I ever!' said Peter. First in Swedish, then in German.

Julia introduced the two new taskforce members to each other: 'This is Bosse Boules. And this is Peter the Small. Shake hands, you two, and then we'll get going.'

The trio carried on towards the town hall. Julia was feeling pleased with her morning so far, even if she hadn't solved the problem of the two hundred parking spaces.

As they walked, Peter explained why he spoke fluent German. 'My mum's from Germany. My parents met at a medical conference in Bonn. I don't know exactly what happened there, but my dad brought my mum back to Sweden with him. And then, not long before the factory closed, they thought they should bring me up *in the fresh air*, so they moved out of Stockholm and came here.'

'I expect the air is plenty fresh enough at the top of Everest,' said Bosse Boules.

'Horribly thin, though,' Peter the Small pointed out. 'Anyway, I think they regretted it. They have to commute to the Karolinska hospital in Stockholm every day. I'm home alone quite a lot, but that's okay. Except in the holidays.'

'Don't you have any friends?' asked Julia.

'Oh yes, I do: three best friends,' said Peter. 'Two of them live in Stockholm now, and one in Uppsala.'

The trio had almost reached the centre of Halstaholm by now. They passed the closed Sound & Vision shop and the equally closed bookshop. As they were going by the not-yet-closed pharmacy, an older lady with a Zimmer frame stepped out of the door.

'Oh look, it's the new madam mayor,' said the lady. 'I didn't know you had a family.'

'Morning, Mrs Johansson!' said Julia. 'You can forget the family thing, though. I'm still single. And really, we've known each other forever: please just call me Julia.'

'Single?' said Mrs Johansson. 'But surely these are your husband and son?'

'Except I'm lucky enough to be married to my own wife,' said Bosse Boules. 'She works in Stockholm, like everyone else round here, it seems.'

'And I'm my mum and dad's son, not the mayor's,' said Peter the Small.

'Oh, I see that now,' said Mrs Johansson. 'But you're still young and pretty, Julia. There's always hope!'

'We want to get the tyre factory back up and running first,' Bosse Boules put in, from which Julia concluded that he really was incapable of keeping his mouth shut.

'It's going to be a German bed factory,' added Peter the Small, who clearly wasn't any better at it.

Something occurred to Julia. 'Mrs Johansson, you know Börje Bolmgren, don't you, who lives on the hill behind the factory?'

'That rascal?' said Mrs Johansson. 'I've had to give him many a clip round the ear in my time, believe you me.'

'But he must be over sixty now,' said Julia.

'He'll always be ten years old to me,' Mrs Johansson retorted.

'It's a good age,' said Peter the Small.

When Julia Bäck walked into the town hall a short while later, she was able to present her full taskforce to Harriet at reception.

'You made short work of that,' said the odd-job woman, sounding impressed. 'Welcome, all of you. Come on in, I'll bring some coffee up in a minute. Mrs Johansson can take the lift.'

'Is there any juice?' asked Peter the Small.

CHAPTER 7

Division of labour

After a successful first meeting, the mayor instructed her taskforce to assemble again at ten the following morning. They arrived punctually, including Harriet, who had hung a 'BACK SOON' sign on the door of the town hall.

'Just for appearances,' she explained. 'We never get any visitors. People who want to complain do it by email now. Not like the old days, when you could have a proper stand-up row with people.'

Then she reflected on what she had actually meant by the old days, and added with a shrug: 'Although back then, there wasn't so much reason to row with anyone.'

Each member of the taskforce was allocated their particular role. Mrs Johansson and her Zimmer frame had to get into Bolmgren's house to negotiate with him. The council needed his house and land.

'When will he have to move out?' asked Mrs Johansson.

'Not before tomorrow,' said Julia. 'Thursday morning at the latest.'

'And what can I offer him in return? Not that he deserves anything, the yob.'

And she told them the story of her time, as a young woman, working in the youth centre next door to the school, where that cheeky brat Bolmgren had hung around. He had been the worst of the lot.

'He stole erasers – a whole bunch of them,' Mrs Johansson said. 'But I got wise to him, and he's been petrified of me ever since.'

Julia admitted that rubber thieves did deserve to be punished, but fifty-five years later the taskforce might be better off forgetting about it and looking ahead. Unfortunately, she still didn't have the faintest idea where the old man from the hill would go if they took his house away.

'I think he's lived there all his life,' said Mrs Johansson. 'Rubber thief or not, he won't like the idea of his family home having to make way for a car park.'

'Well, just go and talk to him for now, and we'll see. There's still plenty of time,' said Julia.

'A day and a half,' said Mrs Johansson. 'All the time in the world.'

Next, Julia handed out the other tasks. First to Harriet: the mayor had a special job for her.

'The boss of Traumbett's Scandi division is coming with his family apparently,' she explained.

'How old are his wife and children?' asked Harriet, who already had an idea where the mayor was going with this. 'And how many are there?'

'Just the one wife, I expect – but I'm afraid I don't know how many children or what ages they are.'

Harriet suggested a little welcome gift for Mrs Kaltenbacher couldn't hurt. The children would be more difficult if she didn't know whether they were five, fifteen or twenty-five. Or how many and what gender they were.

Julia had to admit she was right.

'On the phone, Kaltenbacher didn't sound that old. So his wife is probably going to be somewhere between forty and sixty,' the mayor reasoned.

Harriet promised to do her best. She had an idea in mind already, a gift with a feminine touch. It was a shame that Harrods was in London and not Halstaholm, but she'd find *something*.

Then it occurred to her that at some time in the eighties, she had been to an international business conference in the town.

'They put up flags from all over the world. One of them must have been the German flag, mustn't it? They're probably still around here somewhere, cluttering up a storage room – shall I have a look?'

Julia loved her receptionist! Harriet had understood the beauty-contest thing perfectly.

'What about me?' asked Peter the Small.

'And me?' Bosse Boules added.

They both wanted to be given important tasks, too.

Julia thought for a minute.

Konrad Kaltenbacher was the head of a multi-billion-euro company and wanted to move abroad with his family. The least they could expect was a presentable roof over their heads.

'I mean, he *is* a doctor and everything, not some random paint salesman.'

'My brother's a paint salesman,' said Bosse. 'He lives in a two-bedroom flat in Sundsvall and doesn't seem interested in moving here.'

'No one is,' said Mrs Johansson.

Julia asked them not to interrupt her train of thought. She worried that a deputy CEO with a penchant for luxury villas could be lured away to Lidingö or Djursholm. They were nice and close to the factory, as well. The Stockholm factory.

'Maybe Bolmgren's cabin will be available?' Peter the Small wondered aloud. 'I just mean, you wouldn't have a very long commute if you lived there.'

Julia wasn't sure if this was supposed to be a joke so answered in a neutral tone: 'Bolmgren's hut is eighty square metres at most, needs a lot of work, and anyway, it's going to become a parking space before long.'

It might have to be a new-build, then. On an exclusive lakeside plot, perhaps.

'I don't think the local development plan would permit that,' said Bosse Boules.

'I know for certain it won't,' said Harriet.

Julia remembered that Halstaholm had in fact once employed a town planner, though like most of the other council employees he had been made redundant in the last round of cuts.

'Things planned in the past can surely be re-planned?' she said. 'Otherwise Germany would still be a collection of small independent states, and in Sweden we'd still be driving on the left, to name just a couple of examples.'

Bosse volunteered to take on the role of unofficial town planner; many moons ago he had got top marks in art at school, and he was good at drawing maps. Although there was absolutely zero chance of everything being agreed by the time the German had come to a decision. 'The district council spends ages mulling over planning applications, doesn't it? And then the designs get sent back into the approval process, and then back to the council for agreement, and so on.'

'I have a solution to that,' said Harriet. 'Vesna Slavic!'

At the sound of the name, Mrs Johansson pricked up her ears. 'Sorry, but that old lady is so completely gaga we had to throw her out of the pensioners' association. Which is saying something!'

'I know,' said Harriet. 'That's my point.'

At ninety years old, Mrs Slavic had been on the district council since time immemorial. No one could remember how long exactly, least of all Mrs Slavic. Harriet told them that Torsten Blomquist, Julia's predecessor, had once made use of this when time was of the essence and he wanted to push something through. A trick that could surely be repeated.

'Tell us more, dear Harriet,' Julia said, intrigued.

If Bosse got a move on, redrew Halstaholm, and slipped the sketch to Harriet, she could pass it off as an old council motion that had been put forward by Vesna Slavic two or three years ago.

'At your next council meeting, Julia, you could just refer to it, and say the decision is long overdue. Vesna is senile, the others are tired – and dreadful new-boy Eriksson won't know what's going on. It'll be waved through in thirty seconds.'

'I'll get drawing now!' said Bosse eagerly. 'A six-thousand-square-metre lakeside plot, right?'

'And me?' asked Peter the Small.

Julia thought for a minute.

'With a bit of luck, we'll have the factory, the loading bays and some impressive accommodation to offer,' she counted off on her fingers. 'So all we need is to revamp the whole of Halstaholm. And provide a school for the children. How many people at your school can speak German, Peter? Apart from you and the German teacher?'

'The German teacher left last year. His wife got a job in Malmö, in a museum or something.'

That wasn't good. Their competitors in Stockholm had a whole German school to offer. In prestigious Östermalm as well.

'I'm not sure I know the word you just said,' put in Peter the Small. 'But we can be just as pristeejus as people in Stockholm, can't we?'

'You mean open a German school in Halstaholm, without any teachers who can speak German?' Mrs Johansson asked.

'Excellent idea!' said the mayor, clapping her hands together.

After all, the headteacher of Halsta School, Gunilla Malm, was a born-and-bred Halstaholmer, and her heart was in the right place.

'I'll talk to the headteacher, and see what she says,' said Peter the Small. 'That will also give me a chance to explain why I wasn't back in school this morning with everyone else, before she phones my parents.'

That would have to do for the time being. Julia reminded Peter the Small to treat all information about Traumbett as strictly confidential until further notice.

'Secret, you mean?' said Peter the Small, who didn't like unnecessarily long words.

CHAPTER 8

The consultant who overslept

Kenneth Carlander woke up when his alarm didn't go off. He had forgotten to set it again the night before; something had distracted him. All the same, his subconscious still told him to open his eyes.

'Urrghhh,' he went.

He sat on the edge of the bed to collect his thoughts. This was only partly successful.

Then he saw a half-finished glass of whisky on the bedside table. He grabbed the drink and knocked it back.

'Better already!' he said, and looked at the clock.

Dammit, now he really had to hurry.

'Good morning,' said someone behind him. Two eyes peeked out from under the covers on the other side of the bed.

The consultant had forgotten about them.

'Are you still here?' he said.

'Looks like it,' said the eyes.

'Could you do something about that asap, please? I'm very important and I have an important meeting, so it's incredibly important that I'm not late for it.'

It took Kenneth another few minutes to get rid of the eyes' owner, whoever she was, but then he was able to have a quick shave, wet his hair and comb it, squeeze some toothpaste into his mouth and get into his favourite Armani suit, in which he not only felt but *was* invincible.

Lastly he chugged down the remains of the unknown woman's red wine before rushing down the stairs to hail a passing taxi. That was usually the quickest way to get across the city.

To his chagrin, the old lady next door caused an additional delay, wheezing up the stairs with her stupid dachshund.

'Fuckssake, do us all a favour and take the lift!' he roared at her, as she made every effort not to get in the management consultant's way. 'Lame old women have no business being on the stairs!'

He soon managed to flag down a car and hop into the back.

'City Hall, please! I'm in a hurry!'

The taxi driver explained that Strandvägen was closed, so he'd have to take Sturegatan via Karlavägen.

'I don't care how you get there, as long as you do it quickly!'

The driver was around sixty, and this was not his first rodeo. 'Nothing has been quick in central Stockholm since 1978, but I'll do my best.'

And obviously, the traffic was slow.

When the clock reached a sufficient number of minutes past nine, the consultant's phone rang. Ingela bloody Franzén, of course it was.

'Kenneth Carlander here, what can I do for you?'

'Don't play any dumber than you are,' she barked. 'I'm sitting here waiting, with our eight-hundred-jobs German. Where the hell are you?'

'In a taxi – they're digging up the whole city, the driver had to take a diversion via Helsingfors or somewhere. You just entertain the German, I won't be much longer.'

'Entertain? How? Do you want me to sing him a song?'

The member for finance was more fed up with her adviser than ever. And on top of that, she had to tell him off in the most amicable tone she could muster, so that Kaltenbacher wouldn't see how angry she was.

'I don't know,' said Carlander. 'Talk to him about the royal family or elk hunting or something. The Germans love elk.'

The tip did not go down well.

'I can't think of anything worse than elk – except you, obviously. I'm in charge of Stockholm's finances, and I am standing here like an amateur in front of a man who's prepared to invest *billions* in the city. You promised to land this fish. Where. Are. You?'

Kenneth looked up from his phone to check, but just then the driver pulled up. 'Three hundred krona, please. Cash or card?'

The consultant answered Ingela Franzén: 'I'm here! Give me three minutes!'

And hung up.

They knew him at City Hall, so he was able to sprint past reception and up the stairs. In the corridor outside the member for finance's office, his briefcase went flying as he had to dodge two little girls playing. They leaped aside in fright.

'This isn't a playground, you miserable cockroaches,' Kenneth Carlander hissed.

At last the consultant reached the door. He knocked hurriedly and went in without waiting. Putting on his nicest smile and his best English, he said, 'Doctor Kaltenbacher, it's such a pleasure to finally meet you.'

Konrad Kaltenbacher took the consultant's outstretched hand and replied politely, 'The pleasure is all mine.'

Kenneth Carlander felt the need to apologise. 'What a morning – well, you know how it is. First I was coming down the stairs in my building and a lame old biddy got in my way, and then I was stuck in traffic ... And in the corridor just now two little cockroaches got under my feet. Why can't people keep their brats in order?'

'The cockroaches must have been my daughters,' said Dr Kaltenbacher. 'I'm sorry if they inconvenienced you. How is the old lady?'

'Who?'

'The one on the stairs.'

'Oh, her! Um, fine. Not worth mentioning. Your daughters, yes? Delightful girls!'

Sitting there in her chair, Ingela Franzén looked tormented. She forced a smile, and told her adviser he had better sit down now and try to behave himself for at least ten seconds. Then to Herr Kaltenbacher, in English: 'So, this is my consultant, Kenneth Carlander, the man who made this deal possible. I must apologise for his ... yes, well. But he's a go-getter, you see.'

'Understood,' said Dr Kaltenbacher with an inscrutable smile. Then, to the consultant: 'Mrs Franzén has kindly promised you'll show me the factory site this morning. That would be excellent – right now, if possible. My cockroaches and I would like to see the ABBA museum before we have to rush off.'

The member for finance was still looking unhappy, but her consultant appeared completely unfazed.

'Of course! I'll call a taxi. Only an idiot would drive their own car in this city.'

To which Dr Kaltenbacher replied: 'Then please allow me to be an idiot. My car is parked right outside.'

Konrad Kaltenbacher had only found a parking space outside City Hall because, not being Swedish, he had no idea that this was completely impossible. In his ignorance he had left his car in a bay meant for motorbikes – as if any of those would be out on the roads of the Swedish capital in late October. It had resulted in a yellow slip under one of his windscreen wipers. The consultant snatched up the parking ticket and stuck it in his pocket.

'What was that?' the German enquired innocently.

'Nothing I can't take care of. I have my contacts, you know,' said Carlander.

The twins Maren and Marie were not at all happy in the back seat. Their first encounter with the angry man in the front with Papa was still fresh in their minds. But they understood that their father was doing some important business negotiations here, and they weren't going to make his work unnecessarily difficult.

Still, they were only nine years old, and when the group walked into the huge, almost empty factory hall in Frihamnen, they started testing out the echo:

'Hello, hello! HSV!' Maren cried.

'Hello, Heidi Klum!' called her sister.

Their voices bounced back from the walls.

Next, while their papa was talking to the peculiar Swede, the twins decided to play leapfrog over the abandoned industrial vacuum cleaner on the factory floor.

Both of these things made Kenneth Carlander nervous. In bad schoolboy German he called out to the girls that the vacuum cleaner was an expensive piece of equipment and they should control themselves. But since he didn't know what 'vacuum cleaner' was in German, the sentence that came out of his mouth was not altogether comprehensible.

'The girls can speak English, Mr Carlander,' Konrad Kaltenbacher said calmly. 'And I don't know for sure, but they'd probably even understand the word cockroach if you wanted to use it.'

The morning's dose of whisky and red wine was slowly exiting the management consultant's bloodstream, and the situation was starting to feel uncomfortable: 'I didn't mean ... it's just that this equipment is expensive ... of course the girls can ...'

Konrad smiled. 'I'm extremely satisfied with the production hall,' he said. 'Would you now be so good as to show me the car park and the garage, and perhaps answer a few questions regarding power, water, et cetera?'

'But of course!' said the consultant.

In his hurry, he had forgotten about the electricity and water issue, but he was sure he could guesstimate some figures.

When the tour was finished, Konrad Kaltenbacher asked the girls to hop into the car and he got back behind the wheel. He closed the door, opened the window and informed the consultant standing outside that the building, the location and the parking were very much in line with his expectations.

'The girls and I have another trip out here planned in around two weeks. If we decide to take up your offer, we'll have to think about schools, accommodation and so on.'

'Does that mean we can sign a contract when you come back?' said Kenneth Carlander, passing his business card through the car window.

'First and foremost, it means you have two weeks to answer my questions about electricity, water, and the options for modifying and extending. Your answers so far have been rather vague, don't you think?'

The consultant cursed himself for picking up that slut the previous evening instead of doing any work, but he could hardly say that to old Franzén in City Hall. And certainly not to this German.

'I will go through the figures again thoroughly, Herr Doctor Kaltenbacher, I promise,' he said. 'I can text you the info directly if you like – you've got my card, but I don't think I have yours?'

'No, you haven't. Have a nice day, Mr Carlander, and I look forward to our next meeting,' replied Konrad Kaltenbacher, who had no intention of exchanging text messages with the Swedish consultant.

He rolled up the car window and drove away, leaving the management consultant standing in a godforsaken industrial estate on the outskirts of Stockholm.

'And how do I get back from here?' Carlander shouted after the black Audi. 'Bloody German!'

He had no choice but to call yet another taxi.

CHAPTER 9

The day before: Halstaholm needs a makeover

Peter the Small found the headteacher, Gunilla Malm, exactly where he thought she'd be: in the headteacher's office.

'Peter!' she said. 'How nice that you've found the time to drop in, before I set Interpol on you.'

In good old Halstaholm tradition, everyone at school called each other by their first names, all the way up to the head.

Peter thanked her for not telling his parents, before explaining that he had come to school on urgent business.

'But not to acquire knowledge?' Gunilla Malm asked in surprise.

'Something much more important,' Peter assured her. 'I have contrafunctional information for you.'

'Contrafunctional?'

'Secret, in other words.'

'You mean confidential.'

Peter shrugged. Why did these long words have to exist when they all meant something that could be said much more simply? He decided to get straight to the point, and prefaced it only with, 'The confidentical information mustn't leave this room!'

'Oh!' said the headteacher. 'That does sound serious.'

The boy nodded and told her that he was a member of the mayor's new taskforce. The very next day, a German businessman whose multi-billion-euro company made beds was coming to Halstaholm to look at the old tyre factory.

'Traumbett?' the headteacher asked.

'How did you know?'

'There aren't that many huge German bed manufacturers to choose from. Anyway, I read that they're planning to open a branch in Stockholm.'

'Well, we thought they'd be better off in Halstaholm.'

'That would be fantastic!' the headteacher exclaimed. 'In the old tyre factory?'

Delighted with this contrafunctional and confidential information, she leaped up and went to the large window, letting her gaze roam over the view of the park and – in spirit – to the Halstadäck factory site beyond.

'I was born in this town, Peter,' she said in melancholy, longing tones. 'I had my first kiss down there in that park …'

'Whoa, Headteacher Gunilla,' the boy said, 'I don't need to know all that.'

Gunilla Malm turned to him with a smile.

'Forgive me. All I'm trying to say is: I will do everything I can to get Traumbett to choose us and save our Halstaholm.'

She regained her composure.

'Did you really just say you're on a town taskforce? You do know you're a child, don't you?'

Peter dismissed the comment with a wave of his hand. This wasn't the time to get bogged down in details.

'I'm here on behalf of the mayor herself. We need to start a new school, a German one!'

The headteacher wasn't sure what she had been expecting, but it definitely wasn't that. First, you couldn't just open and close schools willy-nilly. There were inspections, and an education authority … and then the district council had to make a decision on it.

'That's not a problem: Vesna Slavic can make it so it looks like the council approved it ages ago,' said Peter.

'Who?' asked Gunilla Malm, without waiting for an answer. She could see more obstacles ahead than just the matter of permission.

'And second, I don't have a single German teacher.'

'Well, I have an idea,' said Peter the Small.

* * *

It had begun to rain and so Mrs Johansson wouldn't be able to make it all the way up the hill to Bolmgren's house, at least not without an umbrella. Which she couldn't hold because she needed both hands for the Zimmer frame.

'I'll come with you,' Julia offered.

'Stay in the background, though,' said Mrs Johansson. 'I know how to deal with that little tyke.'

When the old lady and the young mayor had gone, Bosse Boules spread out a large map of the town on Julia's desk. He concentrated on the area by the lake, and began to draw in some changes and additions.

'An access road here ... connection to the water main and sewage system here ...'

He drew away happily, zeroing in on the lakeside. All that remained was to divide the land into building plots. Eight should be enough for now; they would just have to add to the plan again later, when people started moving back.

He made the plot closest to Lake Halsta the largest of all, then surveyed his work with satisfaction: 'If my calculations are right, you're getting a top-notch view of the sunset over the lake, Herr Doctor Kaltenbacher. What's that you say? A private jetty? Hmm, that would be in breach of the regulations, but I'll see what I can do.'

And he drew one in.

* * *

With the help of the grabber tool she always carried with her, Mrs Johansson knocked energetically on Börje Bolmgren's door.

'Who's there?' came a grumpy and no longer very youthful voice from the other side. 'I don't need anything.'

'Oh yes you do!' barked Mrs Johansson. 'You need a thorough beating for all those erasers you stole from the youth centre! Open up this minute and maybe you'll escape with your hide intact.'

'Mrs Johansson?' asked the voice, suddenly mousy. 'No, please, Mrs Johansson, that was fifty years ago …'

'Fifty-five. Open up, I said!'

Old Bolmgren dared not resist.

Julia introduced herself: 'Hello, Mr Bolmgren. I'm Julia Bäck, the new mayor. As I understand it, you already have the pleasure of Mrs Johansson's acquaintance. Could we trouble you for a cup of coffee? There are a few things we'd like to discuss with you.'

Bolmgren stepped aside and let the two women in.

'Is this really about those rubbers?' he called anxiously after them.

'Don't pretend to be any stupider than you already are,' said Mrs Johansson. 'Go on, get some coffee on.'

* * *

Headteacher Gunilla walked into the staffroom. There they all were, with their lunchboxes.

'Good lunch?' she asked them.

'Yes, thanks,' said Mr Hedlund, who took the opportunity to add some current, factual information. 'We're a bit stretched since our German teacher moved to Malmö, but I think we've got the timetable covered now.'

'Speaking of German,' said Gunilla Malm, 'I've got Peter Bengtsson here, from 4C. You all know him, don't you?'

The teachers nodded.

'Would you like to take the floor, Peter?' the headteacher asked.

'Thank you,' said Peter, taking two steps forward. 'First, which of you did advanced German at school?'

Three men and one woman raised tentative hands. Peter nodded. 'Mr Hedlund, Mr Almqvist, Mrs Bergman and Mr Skoogh. That will have to do.'

'But I don't remember much of it,' said Mrs Bergman, the eldest of the four. 'It was such a long time ago. May I ask what this is about?'

'We want to open a German school in time for the start of the new school year next autumn. You've got till then to become fluent in the world's most beautiful language.'

The four great hopes looked just as horrified by this as the rest of the staff did.

'And who is going to teach us German?' asked Mr Almqvist.

'I am,' said Peter the Small. 'Two hours, twice a week, with regular homework. And there will be no gum-chewing in class, and no phones allowed.'

Headteacher Gunilla turned a warm smile on her staff and the ten-year-old at her side, before adding: 'The information you have just received is top secret. If that's all, Peter, perhaps we should leave my colleagues here to their lunch-break. You might just have thrown their planning into some disarray.'

'That's all,' said Peter.

But Mr Almqvist, like the others who were in the same boat, had questions.

'May I ask why?' he said.

'Yes, you may,' said Peter. 'But I can't tell you. It has to stay confidential.'

'Secret, in other words,' said Headteacher Gunilla, now captivated by the possibility of saving the town. 'Come on, Peter, I have an idea. I think I know how to finally get rid of Günter Grass.'

* * *

Börje Bolmgren was sitting at his kitchen table with a cup of coffee. Mrs Johansson perched opposite him on her walker. The mayor paced restlessly around the room.

'Five hundred thousand for the house and land ... well, that actually does seem like a fair price,' Bolmgren mused. 'Only, where will I move to?'

Halstaholm is short of a lot of things,' said Mrs Johansson, 'but not empty houses.'

Still, the old man was very sad.

'Look, I know this place is an old hovel, but it's *my* hovel, and I've lived here all my life. I just wouldn't feel right in—'

'Did you used to be a cook?' the mayor interrupted, having spotted a photo on the kitchen wall. It had seen better days: the man in the picture wearing the chef's hat was a much younger version of the old man sitting at the kitchen table.

Bolmgren looked up from the tabletop. 'A chef,' he said. 'You're too young to remember. I had the Halsta Husman down on the ring road. It used to be booked solid every Friday and Saturday. Herring with mashed potato and a glass of red wine for ninety-nine krona. Meatballs, potatoes, lingonberries and a large beer for ninety-nine as well.'

'Sounds delicious,' said Julia, an idea forming in her mind.

Bolmgren went on: 'Then the tyre factory closed down. I had my biggest week ever, record profits, because all the people who were suddenly unemployed came in to drown their sorrows. But once they sobered up, they didn't come back. They couldn't afford it any more.'

'Do you miss being a cook?' asked Julia – step one of the idea she'd just come up with. She returned to the table and sat down.

'Chef,' Bolmgren insisted. 'I think I was pretty good at it, when the restaurant was doing well.'

'Can you do Wienerschnitzel and all that sort of thing?'

'All what sort of thing?'

'You know, German food.'

'Wienerschnitzel is Austrian, isn't it?'

'Forget the Wiener bit, then. Can you do schnitzel and that sort of thing?'

'You bet!'

* * *

For a great many years, a bust of Günter Grass had resided in Headteacher Gunilla's living room. It had been a wedding present from her husband to commemorate their first meeting at a mutual friend's book club, where they had discovered how much they both loved *The Tin Drum*: so much, in fact, that it wasn't long before they loved each other, as well.

Günter had been hanging around in their house ever since, on a pedestal. Gunilla would have gladly got rid of him long ago, because he didn't look like he was in an especially good mood. But she didn't want to upset her husband.

However, now that the future of Halstaholm was at stake, everyone had to contribute. Even if that contribution was grumpy Günter.

When the headteacher and her student arrived at the town's library with Günter in a wheelbarrow pushed by Gunilla, and Peter holding an umbrella over the German author, they were met at the door by Halstaholm's librarian.

'Hello, sister dear!' said Gunilla, setting the wheelbarrow down. 'This is Peter from the district council, and this is Günter – you know him already.'

The librarian, who happened to be the headteacher's little sister, had already been brought partly up to speed on recent developments. But she was still surprised by the ten-year-old's introduction.

'Peter from the district council?' she asked.

'I'm on the town taskforce, when I'm not teaching teachers German,' Peter the Small replied.

'Understood,' said the librarian with a smile. In these strange times, what she had just heard was probably no stranger than all the rest of it. 'I think we'll put Günter up here, then you'll get a good view of him from the street. Do you think I should decorate the big window in German colours, too? I can put everything I have in German out on display. Sometimes we have a theme – maybe this calls for a *German Week*?'

Just then, Mrs Johansson, Julia Bäck and old Bolmgren came past on their way to the town hall.

'Hello there,' said Julia. 'Who's this?'

'His name is Günter,' said Peter. 'He's a German, and Gunilla says he won the Nobel Prize for Literature.'

'Brilliant!' cried the mayor.

'We're planning a German Week as well,' the librarian added.

'Do you think you can have it all planned by tomorrow?'

* * *

Julia Bäck, Mrs Johansson, old Bolmgren and Peter the Small walked (or shuffled, respectively) into the town hall. Harriet, who was knitting behind the reception desk, looked pleased to have some company.

'Welcome, all of you!' she said. 'Oh, and here's Börje Bolmgren – long time no see.'

Bolmgren said he seemed to remember that they had last met in their final year at school, when she'd given him the brush-off at the prom.

'Oh dear,' said Harriet. 'I must have had a blister on my foot or something. Half a century later the memory has faded a little.'

'Or maybe you just didn't want to dance with rascals?' Mrs Johansson speculated.

'It was one rubber, just that one time!' Bolmgren protested.

'It was at least five,' Mrs Johansson shot back.

'Let's put Bolmgren's criminal past behind us once and for all!' urged the mayor, putting an end to the verbal sparring. 'The matter at hand is that he would like to go back to work as a cook, with the council's support.'

'Chef,' said Bolmgren.

'And?' said Harriet.

'He's about to open a German beerhall in a suitable council-owned property. For the time being, he's going to live there, as well, which I'm sure contravenes some law or regulation or other, but we can't let that stop us right now.'

Harriet nodded and understood. So they were going to swap Bolmgren's house and land for a property in the centre of town where he could take up his profession again. The only problem was that the council didn't have all that much property left.

'Your predecessor Torsten sold most of it off to help balance the budget. Of course, we still have the library …'

'We mustn't touch that,' said Peter the Small. 'It has German Week starting tomorrow.'

'What else?' Harriet wondered aloud. 'There's the swimming pool, which that awful Hasse Eriksson wants to bring back to life.'

The pool sounded good, said Bolmgren. It was in the perfect position on the high street to welcome anyone coming in from Stockholm. Its interior would need a little reconfiguring but the ex-rubber-thief took pride in his DIY skills.

'That's settled, then!' said the mayor, resolutely. 'Can you draw up the sale contract, Harriet?'

The receptionist didn't want to be a spoilsport, but could Julia actually sell off council property just like that? And buy other property, as well?

'Have you thought this through, dear?' she added.

'No,' said the mayor. 'When would I have had time for that?'

So she offered Bolmgren two million on the spot for his hovel on the hill and the land that came with it. A not inconsiderable rise from her initial offer – but in return, she was asking exactly the same price for the swimming pool.

Bolmgren nodded. The pool was large; he'd certainly find enough space for living quarters in there too. The men's changing rooms, maybe.

'There must be a shower there already, in any case,' he said.

It occurred to him that he would need cash to convert the building and install the new kitchen and all the other bits and pieces. 'Then I'll throw in another five hundred thousand for your lawnmower,' said Julia.

'It's thirty years old,' objected Bolmgren.

'That's the price you pay for antiques,' said Mrs Johansson.

In return, however, Julia asked for an instant favour. 'Before anything else, you need to hang a big sign on the front. It should be the first thing the German sets eyes on when he arrives tomorrow.'

'I'll need a name for the restaurant,' said Bolmgren.

'Not restaurant,' said Julia. 'Beerhall.'

'What's swimming pool in German?' asked Mrs Johansson.

'An indoor pool is a *Hallenbad*,' said Peter the Small. 'Though the translation of the Swedish *badhus* would actually be *Badehaus* – bath house.'

'I've got it: The Badehaus Beerhall!' cried Bolmgren, beaming.

At that moment, Bosse Boules came down the stairs from the first floor. He was holding a large roll of paper.

'Hello, everyone,' he called. 'I've redesigned the whole of Halstaholm.'

CHAPTER 10

VIPs from Germany

Julia, Peter the Small, Mrs Johansson and Bosse Boules were standing in an expectant line in front of the old tyre factory. Peter told the others he'd persuaded the headteacher to give classes 4 to 6 the day off lessons so that he could organise a German-Swedish football match on the playing field beside the school.

Julia would have liked to hear more, but there wasn't time.

'Where *is* she?' she wondered, looking around impatiently.

'There!' said Bosse.

Pedalling as fast as she could, Harriet came racing up on her bicycle, with a prettily wrapped present in the basket and a rolled-up flag on the pannier rack.

'Sorry I'm late – there were so many flags in the storeroom I almost picked up the Belgian one by mistake. This must be right, though.'

She handed the length of fabric to Bosse, who ran off to hoist it up the flagpole. The German couldn't be more than twenty minutes away now.

'And this is for the wife,' Harriet went on.

'Whose wife?' Peter asked.

'Frau Kaltenbacher,' Julia explained. 'Unfortunately, we don't know how old she is.' Then, turning to her assistant: 'So what is she getting?'

'Well, there wasn't a great deal of choice in town,' Harriet began apologetically. 'But I managed to find this, it's a wickedly expensive face cream. It should make her look ten years younger the first time she uses it.'

Julia nodded approvingly. You couldn't go wrong with face cream.

'So now I think it might be best if you all make yourselves scarce and I welcome the Kaltenbacher family alone.' And to Bosse Boules: 'We'll stay in touch by phone.'

Bosse and the others nodded. Mrs Johansson announced that she had given the pensioners' association a special mission that morning, and had to go and see if they had done their work properly.

'What work?' the mayor enquired.

'Oh, nothing special. We're just jazzing up the roundabout a bit.'

'I'll be ready with the remote control, then,' said Bosse Boules. 'And I'll wait for the green light from you, Julia.'

'What are you planning?' asked Mrs Johansson.

'Oh, nothing special,' said the young mayor.

* * *

Konrad Kaltenbacher was in a good mood. The previous day he'd been shown around a perfect piece of real estate for Traumbett's planned Scandinavian campaign. Everything had been first class, except maybe the reception from that management consultant, who seemed quite chaotic. It had been almost painful to watch the member for finance getting so embarrassed on his behalf. On top of which, he managed to be horrible to the girls.

All things considered, though, Konrad wasn't going to factor the charmless middle-man into the decision. He prided himself on being more professional than that.

His buoyant mood was also partly thanks to the winding country road that led out to remote Halstaholm. It was so much fun to drive. And it was lined with fields and trees in glowing autumnal reds and yellows. Plus, the sun was shining!

Best of all, Maren and Marie were having proper fun in the back, which was infectious. They were currently singing along to ABBA karaoke. Swedish music felt even better in Sweden. It was incredible that the pop group kept its appeal for each new generation. The ABBA museum the day before had been the girls' suggestion.

According to the satnav, they would reach Halstaholm and the tyre factory at two fifty-eight. Konrad decided to speed up a little. One thing he had in common with the Swedes was that three o'clock on the dot meant three on the dot. The Swedes in general, that was, with the exception of this Carlander fellow the day before. Was it his imagination, or had he actually smelled alcohol on the consultant's breath when he arrived?

It looked like they had reached their destination. A blue sign with white lettering announced: *Halstaholm*. But what was this?

Konrad slowed down slightly.

Below the town sign, someone had hung another, blue-painted wooden one with pretty lettering – though handwritten, this time – that read:

Wilkommen! In German!

Konrad Kaltenbacher smiled.

'Look, girls. Julia Bäck is welcoming us in our own language! Isn't that nice?'

The twins turned off 'The Winner Takes It All' and looked out of the tinted window. They spotted what their papa had seen and laughed approvingly.

Then Papa Konrad's eye lit on something else: *Badehaus Beerhall – opening soon!* More German!

'Oh! You love beer, Papa!' cried Maren in delight.

'Düsseldorfer Altbier,' said Marie, more specifically.

Konrad chuckled. The girls knew what he liked.

'What's that over there?' asked Maren.

She had spotted a bust of an old man, but what had really caught her eye was the large window behind it decorated in black, red and gold. And a huge number of books. And yet another sign in German: *Deutsche Wochen!*

Konrad Kaltenbacher frowned.

'Now that's going a little *too* far, Julia Bäck,' he said to himself.

Then they came to the little town's first and only roundabout. A sea of flowers erupted from its centre, in the German colours! But that wasn't what made Konrad Kaltenbacher drive a lap of honour around it. Had his eyes deceived him?

No, the road junction had a name:

Angela Merkel Rondell. In German, of course.

Konrad Kaltenbacher drove on, and would have reached the factory at three on the dot, had the girls not cried, 'Papa, look!' from the back seat at that very moment. Beside the town's school, a football pitch bordered the main street, and a match was in progress between girls and boys of about Maren and Marie's age. With around fifty more children in the crowd.

One team was wearing black and white, with sticky-tape stripes of black, red and gold on their chests. The other was in blue and yellow. A giant plywood scoreboard announced who the opposing teams were, and the current state of the match. In German, of course:

SCHWEDEN 4–4 DEUTSCHLAND

Following Peter's instructions, the referee blew the final whistle just as the car with the German numberplate went past. The Germans and Swedes on the pitch embraced each other.

'That's so cool, Papa!' said Maren

'Isn't it!' said Marie.

Completely bonkers, thought Papa Konrad.

Two minutes later, at 3:02, they were there. Konrad Kaltenbacher spotted a lone woman standing at what looked like the main entrance to the disused factory. It had to be Julia Bäck, of course. Younger than he'd imagined her. Pretty. And elegantly dressed. She was holding something in one hand, and with the other she was directing the driver's attention to the flag fluttering in the wind beside her. There was a smile on her face.

Konrad Kaltenbacher got out of the car and walked towards the mayor. Of course, the first thing he did was apologise for being late.

Julia shook his hand. 'Herr Doctor Konrad Kaltenbacher, I presume? You're younger than I expected.'

The German deputy CEO grinned. 'Julia *Ambush* Bäck? So are you, if you don't mind me saying so.'

'Regrettably, the beerhall isn't open yet,' the mayor went on.

'Even so, we've felt surprisingly at home.'

Julia Bäck was making it more difficult for him to say 'thanks, but no thanks' and drive away, as he'd planned. But what must be, must be.

The Audi's two rear doors opened. Julia, who set eyes on Maren first, was quite beside herself. 'Oh! You're just the sweetest thing I've ever seen!' she cried.

Then Marie came to join her sister.

'And there's another one! Who looks exactly the same! Goodness, I think I'm about to faint!'

The girls smiled shyly. Their father could see that Julia Bäck was genuinely entranced – this wasn't just another component of her charm offensive.

The mayor was still holding a gift in her hand.

'But where's your mama? Won't she come out of the car?' she asked.

'Mama is in heaven,' said Maren.

'Oh? And what's she doing there?' Sometimes Julia Bäck could get a little ahead of herself. Especially when she was on edge. A moment later, she realised.

'Oh, I'm so sorry … please accept my apologies … How could I have …' In an attempt to climb out of the hole she had dug herself, Julia handed the face cream to the girls. 'This … this is for you,' she stammered. 'Apparently it takes ten years off you.'

Konrad Kaltenbacher had never seen anyone say and do so many things wrong in such a short space of time.

'Miss Bäck, Maren and Marie are nine! And this …' he pointed up at the flagpole. 'This is the old East German flag.'

Julia saw that everything had misfired. The charm offensive she'd planned might actually have hindered rather than helped her cause.

'Shall we go inside and see the factory before I manage to do something even stupider?' she suggested.

'I'm almost curious as to what that could be,' said Konrad Kaltenbacher – though he said it with a smile.

Julia Bäck put him in a light, cheerful mood, and had done since their first and so far only conversation, the call from the White House. It was a strange feeling. Four years had passed since Konrad last felt light and cheerful.

To his surprise, the factory building was at least as good as the one in Frihamnen – if not better! Higher ceilings, better equipped, with ready-installed doors and ramps for loading and unloading.

While Julia conducted the tour, Maren and Marie had tremendous fun with the two car tyres the clever mayor had rolled over to them.

'Last one to the back wall is an old crab,' said Julia with a smile.

Better a crab than a cockroach, thought Konrad Kaltenbacher.

By the time they stepped outside again, the wind had dropped. Julia was glad of that, because the East German flag wasn't flapping around quite so prominently.

'That's it, then, Doctor Kaltenbacher. Shall we go to my office and sign the contract now?'

Konrad Kaltenbacher had to admit that the building exceeded all his expectations and he didn't regret taking the detour. But: 'I must say, in spite of everything, I am still wondering if there is something not quite right with you, Julia Bäck. If so, it's very charming, but still …'

He was smiling as he spoke. The mayor studied his face. He was friendly, nice-looking and seemed to have a sense of humour. How old must he be? No more than forty, surely?

'There's plenty wrong with me, I will admit. Just ask the fish in my aquarium at home, he knows. Or maybe he's a she? I have no idea. It might be better not to know; he or she doesn't talk, anyway. Autistic, is my guess.'

Konrad Kaltenbacher laughed. Maren and Marie looked up. They couldn't remember when they'd last heard that sound. And it made them like Julia Bäck all the more.

'Thank you very much for the tour, Mrs Mayor,' said Maren.

'It was nice of you to lend us the tyres,' said Marie. Both girls spoke excellent English.

'Oh, don't mention it, girls,' said Julia. 'Shouldn't we use first names, though? All these titles and surnames – doctor and mayor ... we don't really do that in Sweden. Could you just call me Julia?'

Maren and Marie smiled proudly.

'And you, Papa?' said Maren.

Herr Dr Kaltenbacher held out a hand to the Swedish mayor. 'I'm Konrad,' he said.

'And I'm an idiot,' said Julia. 'But it's been a pleasure. Now, about that contract. Do you need a few minutes to think about it?'

Konrad's face grew serious.

'Let me be quite honest, Julia: the factory building is a hundred per cent suitable – at least! Exactly what I'm looking for. But for me it's about more than that. Take the fact that you promised two hundred parking spaces, for instance. And how many are there? Thirty?'

'Twenty-two,' said Julia, discreetly sending the ready-written message from the phone in her pocket. It said: *Now!*

A few seconds later, old Bolmgren's cabin blew up. It was done with Börje's agreement and Bosse Boules's technical know-how. Plus, a certain amount of chemical fertiliser. Everyone involved agreed on the symbolic value of demonstrating their can-do approach in front of the German.

'What in heaven's name was that?' Konrad Kaltenbacher exclaimed.

'Oh, just the overture to the work on the car park,' Julia explained. 'Did you say two hundred spaces would be enough? Are you sure you wouldn't like three hundred?'

The bang had frightened the girls, too. But now they laughed; they thought everything was perfect. They threw their arms around Julia and turned to their father. 'Can we move to Halstaholm, Papa, please?' Maren begged.

'Yes! Please?' Marie agreed.

Papa Konrad almost hated himself for the fact that he was tempted to say yes purely because the mayor had managed to make him laugh. But he had to remain thoroughly professional.

It was better to put the kibosh on the idea sooner rather than later.

'Girls,' he said. 'I admit I'm just as taken with Mayor Bäck – Julia – as you are. And I will admit that the factory is perfect. We've just had a noisy demonstration that there will be plenty of space for loading, unloading and parking. But this is about the future of Traumbett – and our future, as a family.'

He explained the importance of the transport connection to Stockholm and his daughters' schooling. 'I'm sorry, Julia, but I can't move my darlings to a house in the Swedish provinces, where they'll eventually lose their mother tongue. There's a German school in Stockholm, and I expect one in Gothenburg, too. The Gothenburg one is neither here nor there now, but ... the truth is Halstaholm is simply out of the question.'

Julia pretended amazement.

'Oh! You had me worried there, Konrad,' she said. 'I don't know how I forgot to tell you but in September, in time for the next school year, we're opening a German school here in Halstaholm. Places are limited and demand is already high, but ... well, I *am* the mayor, after all, and I'm pretty sure I can get your two in.'

In one way, Konrad was surprised by this, but in another he wasn't; he was starting to realise he shouldn't be surprised by anything Julia came out with.

'And where would we live?' he asked, weakly.

'A lakeside plot with a private beach, evening sun, and a jetty,' said the mayor, beaming and inwardly saluting Bosse Boules. 'Want to drive over and take a look?'

Konrad Kaltenbacher was on the point of capitulating. But there was one more important issue to clear up: the connection to Stockholm.

'Is it true that the new train line is going to run through Halstaholm?' he asked. 'Because if so, Julia, the deal is as good as done.'

Julia caught herself thinking: *Yes, absolutely* – and then she remembered that the government hadn't made its decision yet.

'Ah. Well, Konrad, there are still a few formalities to take care of,' she said. 'But we're option one, and our only competition is option two. Which is far more expensive! And if there's one thing the Swedish government is good at, it's saving money. Come on, let's go and sign.'

Konrad smiled – how many times had he done that today?

'This is what we'll do,' he said. 'I've promised to go and see the Frihamnen people again in two weeks. So that I can look at accommodation options on Lidingö, among other things. And because they still need to send me some figures. If *you* can put a definite government decision on the train line in front of me by then, *I* will have all the documents I need to make my own decision. Do you think you can manage that?'

'But of course, Konrad,' said Julia. She had made it this far – it should be child's play to convince the permanent secretary at the Ministry for Economic Affairs to give her an advance decision.

CHAPTER 11

A troublemaker kicks up a stink

Hasse Eriksson from the Our Halstaholm party was on his way home from Gnesta. He went over there occasionally to visit a lady for a little fun when there wasn't much else going on. Really, she was too limited for his tastes, but she was beautifully buxom, and in possession of certain skills.

Now he was behind the wheel of his thirteen-year-old Mitsubishi, humming contentedly along to a song on the radio.

But what was this?

Someone had hung a sign under the Halstaholm town sign. *Wilkommen!* In German! And there was worse to come: on the front of his beloved swimming pool there was another sign, saying that a bloody *Beerhall* was *opening soon*!

What the hell was happening?

That snake Julia Bäck had been avoiding him for weeks. Enough was enough!

Hasse accelerated and soon reached the town hall. As usual, he took the always-empty disabled parking space right outside the entrance. He got out and strode through the door. That awful receptionist was sitting there, knitting.

'Listen to me, you old baggage!' he said.

'You just try saying old baggage one more time,' snapped Harriet, who was probably even more fed up with him than he was with her.

'I was just on my way home from a business trip—' he began.

'I thought you were unemployed,' Harriet interrupted.

'... and was welcomed to Halstaholm *in German*!'

The receptionist knew what was coming next.

'And then, a few hundred metres further on, I read that our proud municipal pool is being converted into a German beer-hall! What is going on? Have we been invaded by a foreign power?'

Just wait till you see Günter Grass and the Angela Merkel roundabout, thought Harriet.

'Where's the bloody mayor? And what's she doing with my swimming pool?'

Harriet needed to think. 'I see you've parked your car in the disabled space again. Would you mind moving it?'

'What for? Anyone lame and fragile has already moved away, apart from the old Johansson woman, and she just has a walker, not a car.'

While Hasse was working himself into a frenzy, Harriet managed to come up with an answer.

'Now, as you know, I'm not privy to everything that goes on, but I think Bolmgren the chef has been given permission to rent the building while we're waiting for your renovation motion to be shot down for the third time in quick succession.'

'Bolmgren? That bloke who lives on the hill behind the factory?'

Whose house has just been blown up, thought Harriet. Hasse Eriksson would also get wind of that soon enough, of course. The official explanation would be a gas leak.

'Is Julia upstairs now, or not?' the troublemaker asked insistently.

He was just about to march through the glass doors when Harriet got ahead of him and pressed the lock button. Hasse stopped just short of walking head-first into the glass.

'The mayor is in an important meeting. You'll have to make an appointment like everyone else. *After* you've reparked your car.'

Hasse Eriksson left the town hall with a snort. Harriet phoned Julia.

'Our Halstaholm is on the warpath,' she warned.

'Did he see the beerhall sign?' asked Julia.

'Among other things.'

'Is he coming up?'

'I managed to get rid of him. But he'll be back. What should I do? I fobbed him off by saying that Bolmgren had only signed a temporary rental agreement.'

'Well done!' said Julia. 'Do you think you can hide the sale contract with Bolmgren deep enough in the archive that Eriksson will never find it?'

'The principle of transparency is every council's worst enemy,' said Harriet. 'You can rely on me, Julia.'

CHAPTER 12

The consultant and the holiday photos

Lead Member for Finance Ingela Franzén put two and two together and made four.

The first thing was the follow-up call from Konrad Kaltenbacher in Hamburg. They had agreed the details of his next visit. But while the German had spoken highly of Frihamnen, welcoming the idea of meeting at the factory next time instead of in the city, he didn't seem as eager to finalise a contract as he really should have been if he was a hundred per cent positive about moving. He had voiced doubts about whether Kenneth Carlander could actually come up with the figures on power and water he'd asked for. But was that a reason to rule out Frihamnen?

No, it was worse than that: it seemed the competition in Halstaholm had scored points on their own Traumbett site visit. A week ago it had looked like being a mere courtesy call; an opportunity to negotiate a lower price in Stockholm, perhaps.

The phone call prompted Ingela Franzén to google *Halstaholm* and *latest news*. As it turned out, the local paper, *Halsta Nytt* (which almost no one had heard of), had several informative articles on what might be cooking over there. The place had been turned into a regular 'Little Germany' overnight, with the announcement of a new beerhall, a Günter Grass statue, an Angela Merkel roundabout(!) and various other things. According to *Halsta Nytt*'s anonymous sources, the town was on the brink of signing a contract with a major corporation from Hamburg.

It was scarcely credible but from that moment on Halstaholm would have to be regarded as a serious competitor. So Ingela Franzén had ordered her adviser to be in her office that morning at nine sharp.

She was more than annoyed when the snotty little upstart strolled in at a quarter past wearing a baseball cap and a two-day beard.

'Morning, sweetie,' Carlander greeted her. 'Sorry I'm a bit late, it's these bloody roadworks all over the city.'

'It's still Mrs Franzén to you,' she clarified. 'Now sit down and listen, without going via the drinks cabinet.'

Kenneth Carlander, who had been about to do just that, was put off his stride and did as he was told.

'While you were off getting drunk and shagging around, I was thinking about Hamburg, and I did some research,' said Ingela Franzén.

Shocked by her choice of words, Carlander realised that this time things might be serious.

'Go on,' he said.

'Halstaholm is a competitor we need to pay real attention to. The factory building is suitable, the price is clearly laughable, and they've lured the German in by means that are totally beyond you.'

For the first time, Kenneth Carlander began to fear that his management consultant's fee of three million krona could be in danger.

'What, they're going to open their factory out in the sticks? Surrounded by potato fields and wheat and cows and all that stinking manure?'

'Meat, milk and carbohydrates, you mean,' said Ingela Franzén. 'Besides, those potatoes and wheat are the main constituents of all the alcohol you tip down your throat while you're enjoying a steak for dinner. You useless man! Even half the amount of idiocy you just displayed would make you a complete and total idiot.'

Kenneth Carlander had never seen her in such a rage. It almost made her sexy, but only almost. Luckily, he managed to check himself before actually telling her that.

'Mrs Franzén,' he said instead, through gritted teeth, 'leave it to me. No mega corporation in the world is going to set up in a potato field, however low the price might be. Especially not if the viability of that place is completely upended, transport-wise.'

'How do you propose to do that?' said the member for finance, already sounding milder.

'Are you sure you want to know?' asked Carlander, feeling he was gradually getting the situation back under control.

Ingela Franzén was certain she didn't want to know. But what she did want, more than anything, was to survive the next election unscathed. 'I do,' she lied. 'But I'm a very busy woman, so that will have to wait until next time. Now, kindly go and fix this mess, and make sure you stay sober until the deal is in the bag.'

With that, Kenneth Carlander saw that he could make his escape. He tipped his baseball cap and walked out. On his way, he muttered a summary of the meeting into his stubble: 'Stupid tart.'

* * *

While Bosse Boules was making some additional minor modifications to the town planning map (which among other things required an alcohol licence for the former swimming pool), and Peter the Small was giving his first German lesson to his four new pupils from the teaching staff ('What did we say about chewing gum in class, Mr Almqvist?'), and Mrs Johansson was coercing the pensioner brigade into jet-washing the façades of every building in Halstaholm – while all this was going on, the mayor was doggedly pestering permanent secretary Hannes Marklund at the Ministry for Economic Affairs, in an attempt to force him to confirm the new route for the southern main line.

'It's looking good,' said the permanent secretary, 'really good. We'll definitely make a firm decision in the next few days, and the minister will be giving a press conference in a week's time at the latest.'

'Then I'll call again tomorrow,' Julia told him.

'Please don't …' begged the permanent secretary.

'And the next day, until you tell me something concrete. I'm very committed to ensuring my town's survival!'

* * *

Once he'd ended the call with the tenacious mayor of Halstaholm, the permanent secretary was expecting a visit from an old pal. He didn't really have time for that sort of thing, but Kenneth Carlander had piqued his interest the day before with a text message about something 'incredibly cool' he had in the pipeline.

Hannes Marklund had barely hung up the phone when Carlander appeared at his door.

'Hey, you old sea dog! It's been ages!'

The permanent secretary grinned from ear to ear. 'Kenneth! Mate! I'm insanely busy, but when you get in touch, everything else just has to wait.' The permanent secretary shuffled his papers on the new stretch of railway into a pile. 'You said you had something cool in the works? I don't like to be nosy – but, you know, anything that might be helpful to us in the next election ... heh-heh.' Hannes Marklund laughed. With no idea what he was laughing at.

Kenneth Carlander opened his briefcase and fished out a few sheets of paper.

'Ah yes, such great memories ...' he said, casting a glance at the papers in his hand. He was enjoying giving the impression he was just here for a perfectly harmless chat with his old pal. 'So, Hannes, how's it going? You guys are about to decide the new route for the southern main line, right?'

Hannes Marklund still didn't suspect a thing. 'Since when have *you* been interested in railways? You go everywhere in giant limousines – or on business-class flights.'

'Trains are for environmentalist morons,' Kenneth Carlander scoffed. 'My yacht, on the other hand – now that's really something. You wouldn't believe how much diesel it drinks! It's a marvel.'

The permanent secretary pulled a shocked face and closed the door to the corridor.

'Seriously! You can't say those things out loud round here,' he scolded Carlander.

'It's true, though! Remember last summer, when we went out sailing round the archipelago together? We must have got through two hundred litres of diesel at least. And three hundred of champagne!'

Now the consultant was drumming both thumbs on his papers. At the mention of the archipelago trip, Hannes Marklund had begun to feel a little unwell.

'You're deciding between two options, is that right?' asked Carlander.

The permanent secretary looked surprised. 'Are you somehow au fait with the government's future transport strategy?'

Kenneth Carlander waved a hand dismissively. 'Oh, one tries to keep up with these things when necessary. So is it going to be option one or option two?'

This was the exact question the mayor of Halstaholm had asked him just a few minutes ago, and Hannes Marklund had almost let slip their approval for option one. But now that an old pal was asking …

'It's still top secret for a few more days, but we're preparing a press conference to announce option one,' he said. 'It connects more places inland. But don't tell anyone.'

'And what if we went for number two instead?' Carlander asked.

Hannes Marklund took the question as a question rather than a suggestion. 'Oh, well, the coastal option requires a lot more groundwork; there are some marshy areas out there that add about a billion to the cost. And sure, you knock a couple of minutes off the journey time, but as you know, money rules the world.'

'Not like it used to be,' said Kenneth. 'When cock was still king.'

The permanent secretary shot a glance of alarm at the now-closed door. His pal fanned out the papers he'd been holding on Marklund's desk: photos from their archipelago trip fifteen months previously. Their boys' holiday with plenty of girls. All young models in bikinis. Crates and crates of champagne. And photos of Hannes Marklund tipping a full bottle over one of the models, and trying to lick her clean.

Now the permanent secretary was really getting anxious. 'What is all this, Kenneth? I thought we were mates? You can't seriously be saying we have to change the route of the train line, or you'll—' Hannes Marklund didn't finish his sentence.

'But of course we're mates, Hannes!' the consultant assured him. 'If you want to borrow the boat next summer with your wife and your lovely children, all you have to do is ask. But this is *politics*. I want that railway line kept as far from Halstaholm as possible, and you can help me with that, can't you?'

'Shit, Kenneth—' the permanent secretary was croaking, when Carlander interrupted. He had already stood up and was on his way to the door, leaving the trip photos on Hannes Marklund's desk.

'You can keep those as a souvenir. And if you should happen to lose them, don't worry: I've got a lot more where they came from. Much worse ones.'

CHAPTER 13

One or two?

Julia Bäck was as good as her word. She called the permanent secretary every single morning and afternoon for the next week. But Hannes Marklund was not at his desk, or in an important meeting, or had a call on the other line, or wasn't in yet, or had gone home for the day.

Thanks to the Badehaus Beerhall, Günter Grass, the Angela Merkel roundabout, football-playing children, and the rumour of a new German school, the local paper was enjoying an unprecedented rise in circulation, at least since the bloody internet had come along and ruined it all.

Even Sweden's most important daily paper, *Dagens Nyheter*, was printing stories about Halstaholm, suggesting it was competing with the capital for the biggest foreign industrial investment in living memory. Swedish and German media all wanted a comment from Dr Konrad Kaltenbacher Jr, but no one could get past his secretary, Frau Müller, who batted them skilfully away. First, because she was a very skilful operator. And second, because the callers all gave her their real names, and she was confronted with neither a fake Henry Kissinger nor a pseudo-Greta Thunberg.

At home in the Kaltenbacher house, Konrad found himself under constant siege from the twins. They insisted they *loved* Julia, they *loved* her town – and then, one day, they *loved* the plot of land that the mayor had sent photos of. And he mustn't worry about them. If they got to move to Halstaholm instead of that stupid free port in that stupid capital city, they would *love* Sweden, too.

'We can already say loads of Swedish words,' said Maren.

'Oh yes?' said Papa Konrad. 'What are they, if you don't mind me asking?'

The girls readily explained: 'Avicii ... IKEA ... H&M ... Johannes Thingnes Bø ...'

'The biathlete?' said Konrad. 'He's Norwegian. Now finish your dinner and then go and give your teeth a proper clean. You've got school tomorrow.'

The pair flitted off towards the bathroom. And Konrad was left in the kitchen with the washing up. And his thoughts.

Halstaholm really wouldn't be feasible if nothing came of the high-speed rail link to Stockholm. He estimated Traumbett would need five hundred and fifty workers for the first phase, of whom at least fifty would have to be highly qualified, and the majority of them would prefer to keep on living in the capital, where Konrad was planning to recruit them. No one would choose a job that involved an hour's commute by car, or even longer on the bus with a change in Södertälje, no matter what salary he was offering. But a twenty-minute train ride would change everything.

And the lovely Julia had promised! Most importantly, the Swedish government had promised a decision a few days ago. Though the latest update was that they were postponing the planned press conference by a whole week. Why? Was option one becoming option two, and vice versa?

CHAPTER 14

The espionage mission

News of the delayed press conference was very good tidings for Kenneth Carlander. But to be on the safe side, he WhatsApped the permanent secretary, his (probably now former) pal, an even more salacious photo just to make sure Hannes Marklund stayed on task.

The management consultant was feeling pleased with himself. For a moment, it had actually looked like he'd totally screwed up the deal, but now he'd turned things around. In times of war and crisis, he found his best form. And with this second wind in his sails, he decided to pay a visit to Halstaholm and inspect the competition for himself. Incognito, of course. And that tart in City Hall didn't need to know about it, either.

But a feeling of foreboding crept over him when he went online to book a hotel room. There was one available in a Hotel Halsta – and that was it. He had never in his life been so far out into the sticks as on this mission. He doubted the place would even have any phone reception.

* * *

Anyone wanting to visit Halstaholm incognito would be well advised not to rock up in a golden-yellow Porsche, an Armani suit and – on a cold, overcast day in early November – dark sunglasses. In theory, Kenneth Carlander knew all this, but there was a limit to what he would put himself through.

On checking into the hotel, he was informed that the reception desk closed at six in the evening but that the room keys would also open the front door.

'Is there a minibar in the room?' he asked.

'Minibar?' asked the woman on reception.

'Okay, forget that. Where would you advise me to go if I wanted a filet mignon and a Châteauneuf-du-Pape?'

'A shadow what?' said the receptionist, who until eleven years ago had been responsible for purchasing studs for snow tyres at the factory.

Kenneth Carlander sighed. 'For the love of God, where can I get a bite to eat and some booze around here?'

The receptionist beamed. 'Oh right! I recommend Pizzeria Halsta, just up the street from here. But you might want to take off your sunglasses so you don't walk into a lamp-post on the way.'

* * *

There was something in that. He left the sunglasses in the hotel room, and was thus able to avoid the single lamp-post between hotel and pizzeria.

There were plenty of free tables. Well, all the tables were free except two. Kenneth chose the one furthest from another single diner, suspecting him of smelling like a farmyard. Though the second man was still a little too close for his liking, even if he was wearing a blazer. With jeans, but still.

After two beers, the same number of Jägermeisters and half a capricciosa, life was looking much rosier. Perhaps he should mingle with the natives and see what came of it? Carlander raised his glass in the direction of the blazer-and-jeans man and said: 'Cheers! This little town makes a nice first impression.'

The jeans man looked up from his evening paper. There was nothing left in his glass for him to return the toast with. And he didn't look like he wanted to, anyway. 'Nice? Halstaholm is absolutely riddled with corruption!'

Carlander realised at once that he had stumbled straight into a gold mine, and called out to the cook who was standing over by the pizza oven to bring them a couple more beers and the same number of Jägermeisters.

'All right, I've just got to—' the cook began.

'Now!' said Kenneth Carlander.

Five minutes later, the management consultant and the council troublemaker were sitting at the same table. Another half an hour, and Carlander was very much in the picture on most things.

He had clearly hooked a genuine Halstaholm native, and on top of that a fervent political hobbyist. A man who not only felt that Julia Bäck had gone behind his back, but was most probably right. As they grew increasingly intoxicated, Carlander gradually winkled more information out of Hasse Eriksson. The mayor had rented out the old swimming pool, he said, without the council's approval. There were also rumours going around that the school was in the process of being turned into a German institution, and there had been no due democratic process there, either. And students had been playing football outside during lesson time!

Furthermore, a bust had been erected outside the library without planning permission, and the previously nameless, and blameless, village roundabout had been christened Angela Merkel ... According to Hasse Eriksson, that was just the start of a long list of complaints, but first he needed another beer and a Jäger to straighten out his synapses.

It was ten o'clock, and the cook wanted to close up.

'You'll get a thousand-krona tip if you stay open for another half an hour,' offered Kenneth Carlander.

But the cook was more than just a cook; he was the former head of finance for Halstadäck, and had seen something of the world. More pertinently, he knew an Armani suit when he saw one.

'Ten thousand,' he said. 'For an hour. Paid in advance.'

Hasse Eriksson puffed himself up in outrage. This was extortion!

Kenneth Carlander, however, experienced a warm glow. It was like being back home in civilisation, rather than squatting in a potato field chewing on pizza crusts.

'Eight thousand,' he said. 'Including two more beers and two more Jägers. And an hour and half, if we need it.'

The pizza cook agreed to everything except the extra time. 'An hour is my final offer, or I risk losing my licence.'

The management consultant and the cook shook on it.

'Right, where were we?' said Kenneth Carlander to Hasse Eriksson, who couldn't quite believe what had just happened.

CHAPTER 15

Breaking and entering for beginners

The taskforce assembled in the mayor's office. Harriet had hung the 'BACK SOON' sign on the front door and was therefore able to join them as an additional member. It was about time everyone was brought fully up to date, so they could agree on next steps.

Peter the Small reported that he had already given two double lessons of German to his students – that is, the four teachers Gunilla Malm had picked out. Two of them, at least, were making good progress, though Mr Hedlund had trouble knowing when to use the dative or the accusative, and Mrs Bergman had trouble with discipline.

'I mean really, she can't be sitting there in lessons with her phone hidden under the table, appealing against her tax bill!' Peter the Small complained. 'Personal matters should be sorted in your own time!'

Mrs Johansson had no complaints about her pensioners' association. They had cleaned graffiti off walls all over town and swapped the flowers on the Angela Merkel roundabout for plastic lookalikes, which would survive the coming winter. But she did have worrying news for them: the evening before, she had been out with her Zimmer frame getting some fresh air, to help her sleep. And she was just passing the pizzeria, reminiscing about old times …

'Old times?' wondered Peter the Small. 'Did you use to be a pizza chef?'

'No, a curator,' said Mrs Johansson.

Bosse Boules explained to the taskforce member who was too young to know: 'Before she retired, Mrs Johansson was head of Halstaholm's important archaeology museum. And once she was gone, Julia's predecessor decided to sell off the building and send all the old stuff to the Historical Museum in Stockholm. The museum became a pizzeria. A cultural outrage, if you ask me.'

But Mrs Johansson didn't quite share his opinion. 'In my last year there, after the factory had closed, I had an average of two visitors a month. And one of them was my granddaughter, who knew she'd get sweets whenever she showed her face.'

Anyway, Mrs Johansson and her Zimmer frame were in the habit of taking a little detour past the former museum – and yesterday evening, she had seen Hasse Eriksson in there!

'What's so alarming about that?' asked Julia. 'Was he drinking water? If so, we'll have to write to the papers.'

'No, he was having a beer and a chaser, all very normal. But he was sitting with someone from out of town,' said Mrs Johansson.

'How do you know?' said Peter the Small.

'You could tell by the man's clothes, his manicured nails, his haircut and his arrogant smile. He was clearly from Stockholm.'

This piqued Julia Bäck's curiosity.

'Our troublemaker was getting pally with a man from Stockholm?' she said. 'I wonder what they were plotting.'

'It gets worse,' Mrs Johansson went on. 'When you told us about our competitor's plans, you showed us some articles, including an interview with a real estate adviser whose name escapes me now.'

'Kenneth Carlander,' muttered Julia.

'Right! And *that's* who it was.'

Julia asked if she was really sure about that.

Mrs Johansson did not take kindly to this.

'Well, I'm not daft: I knew this Stockholmer wouldn't be spending the night on a park bench, so I called my daughter, who called her friend Alice, who works on the Hotel Halsta reception desk. Hasse Eriksson was *definitely* getting cosy with Consultant Carlander. The man who wants to take Traumbett to Frihamnen!'

The information was as unsettling as it was mysterious.

'That's got to be bad news,' said Julia. 'But what can we do except wait and see what they're up to?'

Harriet cleared her throat. 'I've taken the sale contract between the council and Bolmgren and hidden it in the archive so thoroughly that Hasse Eriksson will never, ever find it. But he mainly won't find it because he's not too bright. If he has outside help, from someone with a proper grasp of the principle of transparency, that might be a risk. Straight after this meeting I'm going to pop back in there and hide it even better.'

Bosse Boules was interested to know how exactly the hiding had been done. Harriet explained that the contract was supposed to be under B for Bolmgren. But with a little free association you could just as easily file it under B for Badehaus or B for Beerhall. The problem then was that it was still under B, no matter how much associating you did. Anyone looking under B would find it.

'So I filed the contract under W for Wienerschnitzel,' said Harriet. 'And now I'm planning to re-file it under the carpet.'

'Under C for carpet?' asked Peter the Small.

'No, just under the carpet.'

Next to report was the unofficial town planner. He and Harriet had looked through the previously approved applications and backdated everything relating to council scrutiny of planning permission, the alcohol licence and that sort of thing, so it could be waved through at the council meeting the next day.

'We attributed everything to Mrs Slavic,' said Bosse Boules. 'But are you sure she won't remember what she proposed and what she didn't?'

'Yes,' said Harriet.

Mrs Johansson confirmed: 'She has trouble remembering her own name. And that's not all! Before we were forced to remove her from the pensioners' association, she tried to wash her underwear in our coffee machine.'

Then it was Julia Bäck's turn. A week ago at least, the permanent secretary at the economic affairs ministry had given her clear hints that the government was intending to go with option one for the new rail line. But then the press conference had suddenly and unexpectedly been postponed by a week. And when the same permanent secretary managed to avoid eighteen phone calls from her in a row, she had jointly googled him and the confounded consultant whom Mrs Johansson had seen last evening in the pizzeria.

'And?' said Mrs Johansson.

'Hannes Marklund and Kenneth Carlander are old pals! There are pictures of the pair of them, all smiles, on a cruise around the Stockholm archipelago last summer. They've got their arms around each other and they're raising glasses of champagne. The pictures aren't particularly revealing, but it's easy to imagine the two of them getting up to all kinds of shenanigans together over the years.'

'You mean Carlander persuaded Marklund, and he in turn persuaded the minister?' asked Mrs Johansson.

'I can't rule it out,' said the mayor. 'Or his efforts at persuasion are still ongoing.'

'What can we do about it?' put in Peter the Small.

'Not a lot,' sighed Harriet.

'Oh no, there's plenty we can do,' said Mrs Johansson.

She had an idea.

For her own sake, Julia hoped the idea wasn't going to be too outlandish. In her first few weeks in office she had already blown up a house, sold off a public building behind the councillors' backs, redirected the district's education strategy without any approval from anyone, given children in compulsory education time off lessons – and secretly had the whole Halstaholm town plan redrawn. All that and more.

'Dare we hope that your plan is totally above board, Mrs Johansson?' she said.

'Hope springs eternal. I was thinking we ought to break into the pizzeria,' said the old lady with the Zimmer frame.

The valiant mayor closed both eyes and then opened them again.

'Breaking and entering is one of the few offences I haven't committed yet,' she said. 'So what the hell.'

CHAPTER 16

The consultant and the useful idiot

To his own surprise, Kenneth Carlander was on time. He was standing outside the front door of the doss house where he had spent the night, waiting for Hasse Eriksson, who had promised him a tour of Halstaholm as an overture to them developing a strategy that would bring about Julia Bäck's downfall.

Or rather, it was Carlander who would have to come up with the strategy, because the Halstaholm native lacked all capacity for that sort of thing. The management consultant had got the measure of Hasse Eriksson in the pizzeria the previous evening. With a useful idiot, you just had to pull the right string to get your own way in any given situation. And so Halstaholm's political attack dog was now convinced it would be better for the town if Traumbett *didn't* open a factory there. Otherwise Julia Bäck would probably end up a local hero, and she and her party would get at least a ninety per cent vote share at the next election. In which case the swimming pool would never be a swimming pool again, and the whole district would be overrun with foreigners. But Hasse Eriksson and his Our Halstaholm party were the future of the region. Before the region could realise that, though, they would have to get the new mayor out of the picture.

That's how you get things done, thought Carlander with satisfaction.

Kenneth put his sunglasses back on and smoothed down his suit. He didn't have to go out looking like the village idiot just because he happened to be among village idiots.

A car pulled up. Hasse Eriksson opened a window and called out, 'Morning! Hop in and let's go! Thanks for yesterday, by the way.'

Hop in? Into a substandard, not exactly new Mitsubishi Colt? Not on your life.

'Let's take my ride,' said Kenneth Carlander. 'It's just round the corner. You'll know it when you see it.'

He wasn't completely stone-cold sober, but he was in fairly good shape after his morning hair-of-the-dog. And everybody knew a lightly tipsy chauffeur was the best driver.

And so the not-completely-stone-cold-sober consultant got behind the wheel of his Porsche, and the troublemaker issued directions from the passenger seat. First, they headed for the library and drove past the bust the mayor had plonked down there without planning permission.

'Who's that supposed to be?' asked Kenneth Carlander.

'Günter Grass,' said Hasse Eriksson.

Getting no immediate reaction, he added, 'Famous German guy.'

'Like Franz Beckenbauer?'

'Something like that.'

They carried on to the Angela Merkel roundabout with its flowerbed in appropriate colours.

'Hasn't she retired?' said Kenneth Carlander.

'I don't know,' said Hasse Eriksson. 'All I know is that Julia Bäck isn't allowed to go renaming streets and junctions whenever she feels like it.'

The consultant could only agree. Well, there it was: now all they had to do was leaf through the statute books and find the right paragraphs. *Misuse of office* maybe? Or *unauthorised assumption of authority* at the very least.

When they reached the tyre factory, the consultant pulled a face. The building was enormous, that was true, and so long that it looked perfect for the needs of a corporation like Traumbett.

Since the mayor's meeting with Herr Dr Kaltenbacher outside the place, Harriet had not only replaced the East German flag with an updated one, but managed to bring the other five flagpoles on the long side of the factory into service as well. Not a bad move, Kenneth had to acknowledge grudgingly, while Hasse Eriksson snorted, 'What objection do they have to the *Swedish* flag, I'd like to know.'

The useful idiot had literally no idea about anything.

'Didn't a house explode somewhere round here?' Carlander asked.

Hasse pointed to the hill, where they could still see the remains of what had once been a red log cabin.

'I looked into the matter,' he said, trying to sound important in front of the Stockholmer. 'The police dismissed it as a gas leak, just like Bolmgren claimed.'

'Bolmgren?'

'The man who's renting the swimming pool all of a sudden, and turning it into a beerhall. A *German* beerhall, if you can believe that.'

Kenneth Carlander thought there were stranger things in the world than a beerhall being German, but he kept that thought to himself.

'Shall we go up there and have a poke about in the rubble?'
'Why?'
'Well, you never know.'

Poking about in what had until recently been old Bolmgren's home turned up the remains of an electric cooker. Who would have an electric cooker if they had a gas supply and therefore, in all likelihood, a gas cooker as well? Two cookers in such a small cabin? Though that didn't mean for sure that it was an arson attack; in a gas explosion, logically the thing that gets truly blown to smithereens is the gas cooker itself.

But one thing at a time. The chain of evidence against the mayor was beginning to take proper shape.

'And now we're going to the school,' Kenneth declared.

'Why?' Hasse Eriksson said again.

'To give the headmaster a bit of a fright. Do you know his name?'

'Gunilla Malm.'

CHAPTER 17

The daily phone call

For a good week now, Julia and Konrad had been talking on the phone every evening. Officially for business reasons, but, with each call, the conversations had grown longer, and quickly gone beyond Traumbett's move to Scandinavia.

Among other things, Julia now knew that Marie and Maren's mother had died four years ago in a car accident, caused by a drunk driver who was six times over the limit. It was so tragic the mayor's stomach tied itself in knots.

Konrad, in turn, now knew that Julia had lived with Magnus for several years, but, like so many others, he had started commuting to Stockholm when he lost his job in Halstaholm. Magnus had begun to stay overnight in the capital more and more, until one day he arrived home with the gift of a fish tank plus one fish, and the confession that he'd been having an affair with someone in Stockholm. But it was over now, he said, and he wanted them to start again.

'That's terrible!' said Konrad. 'What did you do?'

'Kicked the boyfriend out and kept the fish,' said Julia.

The mayor and the deputy CEO also discovered a shared love of Paris. Both laughed heartily at the idea of meeting there in spring, as long as it didn't clash with the opening of the new factory.

But each conversation also contained an unavoidable dose of reality. Konrad said he thought Julia understood that he couldn't just choose Halstaholm if the new train line went elsewhere. They were really warming to each other, Paris or no, but both also knew in their heart of hearts that a company boss in Frihamnen and a mayor in Halstaholm wouldn't commute back and forth to deepen their friendship. With the change in Södertälje and everything.

During their last conversation, Konrad told Julia that he'd spoken to the permanent secretary at the Swedish economic affairs ministry. When Konrad asked him why the press conference had been put back, his answer was quite evasive.

Julia felt she couldn't tell the German any more fibs. She liked him too much. But one tiny little white lie could hardly make things worse than they already were, could it?

And so she made a great show of assuring Konrad that he had nothing to worry about. Next Thursday the two of them would have everything they needed, confirmed in black and white.

Konrad reminded her that he and the girls had a meeting lined up with the management consultant and the member for finance in Frihamnen the very same day.

'That's great!' said Julia, still feigning confidence. 'It will give you the opportunity to say goodbye to them in person. I'm sure they'll appreciate such a mark of respect.'

'And then it'll be straight off to you to sign a contract, you mean?' He laughed.

'Your own jetty, Konrad! You haven't really made it in life until you've got your own jetty!'

CHAPTER 18

Council meeting

Nineteen members sat in their places along both sides of the long table. The twentieth, Julia Bäck, was at its head. The fifth chair on the left side of the table was still empty.

The mayor looked at the clock.

'I say we make a start. Hasse Eriksson seems to be otherwise engaged.'

Just then, the troublemaker burst through the door.

'Some bastard nicked my parking space!'

'Your disabled parking space, you mean? Sit down, please, so we can start – there's a lot to get through on today's agenda.'

It was a long time since Hasse had seen Julia, and now, as if the scales had fallen from his eyes, he realised how attractive she was.

'*Well*, gentlemen, the old goat who used to sit at the head of this table has been replaced by a hot chick!'

'The old goat advised the hot chick to tell the donkey to shut up,' Julia shot back.

And she whizzed through the first few points on the agenda, opening and welcome, establishing the quorum, approving the agenda and the minutes of the last meeting, until she reached the first item that required a vote.

The resourceful mayor brought up an image of the planning map, freshly drawn by Bosse Boules, on the large monitor.

'So you're all familiar with this, except Hasse, who is new here.'

No one was familiar with it at all, but they weren't about to admit that.

'First, I would like to thank Mrs Slavic for the excellent groundwork and well-thought-out proposal. Can we move to a vote?'

Vesna Slavic was almost certain she'd heard someone say her name.

'What have I done now?' she asked, hesitantly.

Julia smiled. 'We all forget things now and then, Vesna. But it's high time the council made a decision on your proposal.'

A smile spread over Vesna Slavic's face.

'When I was a little girl in Belgrade, we were always forgetting to come home on time. Oh dear, how Mama used to scold us …'

The chair of the council thanked the proposer for her clarifying statement.

'So can we come to an agreement on proposal 17.03?'

No one in the room knew what proposal 17.03 contained.

'All those in favour, please raise your hands.'

Nineteen hands went up. The nineteenth belonged to Mrs Slavic, who wasn't sure what was happening but joined in when she saw what everyone else was doing. Twenty hands including Julia's.

'Those against?'

'Hold on, this is all happening too fast for my liking,' said Hasse Eriksson, without raising his hand.

'Twenty in favour, none against, and one abstention,' said Julia, and struck the gavel on the table. 'Let the record show that the councillors have passed the following: the new town plan, the new roundabout, and the renting or lease of the swimming pool, to include an alcohol licence. Any questions, or can we all go home?'

An outraged Hasse Eriksson jumped to his feet. 'How have you packed all that into one vote? This is criminal!'

Julia eyed the troublemaker calmly. 'As I said, you're new, but we won't hold that against you. Still, everyone here has read the small print except you, it seems. Were you too busy parking illegally?'

A few councillors suppressed a giggle; others laughed openly. Mrs Slavic explained that when she was a little girl in Belgrade, *everyone* parked illegally.

But Hasse Eriksson refused to admit defeat.

'You didn't have any planning permission for that statue outside the library, you bloody witch!'

From chick to witch in a matter of minutes. But Julia genuinely hadn't considered planning permission for the bust. That kind of thing was best solved by turning the construction into a mobile installation, surely?

'You do know it's on wheels, right? Anyway, it's a bust, not a statue.'

She made a mental note to phone the librarian straight after the meeting and ask her to put some wheels on Günter Grass.

CHAPTER 19

Night shift

It had been a long day. And then an equally long evening, with the council meeting. And now the night shift awaited her.

Meanwhile, Konrad Kaltenbacher was putting his daughters to bed, since he would be waking them earlier than usual the next morning. The three of them were embarking on another long drive to Stockholm, followed by a night in the Grand Hôtel and a final, decisive meeting the next morning in Frihamnen.

'Halstaholm, Papa,' was the last thing Maren said before her eyes closed.

'That's right,' murmured Marie.

Konrad thought that life was making business unnecessarily difficult for him at the moment. He didn't have a good feeling about the two train line options.

At the same time in Halstaholm, Peter the Small was shovelling meatballs and mashed potato into his mouth.

'You eat meatballs like a real Swede!' his mother told him in German.

'I *am* a real Swede, Mama,' Peter said in the same language, before switching to Swedish: 'At least half as real as Papa and twice as real as you.'

His parents smiled at how well their son had turned out. They felt permanently guilty about work keeping them away from home for such long hours.

'That's your Swedish grandmother's recipe,' said Peter's papa in Swedish. 'I must say, you're doing her memory proud. How many of those meatballs have you had now? Fifteen?'

'I'm a growing boy, Papa!'

What their son didn't tell them was that he was building up his strength in preparation for the night ahead.

His mother said in broken Swedish: 'Papa and I have to go to work very early tomorrow. Are you sure you'll be all right getting yourself up and going to school on your own?'

'But, Mama,' said Peter in German, before switching straight back to Swedish again, 'I do that every morning!' He feigned a yawn, wiped his mouth with his serviette and got up. 'Thank you for dinner, but I have to excuse myself now. It's getting late – I'd better hit the sack.'

'Already?' said his mother. 'Don't forget to …'

'… brush my teeth,' said Peter. He knew his mama.

Up in his room, he waited with the door closed until the rest of the house was quiet. Then he put on warm, dark clothes, rubbed soot on his face, and pocketed a torch before carefully opening the window that looked out over the yard.

He had put up the ladder earlier, long before his parents got home. No one noticed it leaning against the back of the house in the November darkness.

At around the same time a few kilometres away, Bosse Boules was doubting himself even more than usual. He loved his Maja, but tonight's plan called for complete secrecy. The town taskforce was about to try and divert the Swedish government's long-term, nationwide transport strategy. Billions of krona were at stake, and it would affect millions of people for the next hundred years or so.

'A town planning meeting in the middle of the night?' Maja asked. 'You've been busy pretty much round the clock lately.'

But at least she was smiling as she said it. She knew how much his activities for Traumbett meant to him. It was all voluntary, as well.

Bosse avoided answering so he wouldn't have to tell any more lies. Instead, he gave his wife a kiss and left.

They were meeting at the town hall on the stroke of midnight. That was what they had agreed. Bosse was joined by Julia, who arrived in her otherwise little-used Volvo V70. Peter the Small was already there as well.

'Your face is all black – what have you done to it?' asked the mayor.

Peter said he had learned from Netflix that you should blacken your face with soot before going out on military ops at night. Especially if there was a full moon.

'Good idea,' said Julia, thinking that with the heavy, dark rainclouds currently hanging between heaven and earth it was hard to tell whether the moon was full or not.

Only Mrs Johansson was missing. The minutes ticked by: five past, then ten past. She was never late!

Eventually they heard the unmistakable squeak of her Zimmer frame, quite a while before she herself emerged from the shadows.

'I'm very sorry, I had to hunt high and low for my husband's long johns before I finally found them!'

'Couldn't you just have asked him?' said Peter the Small.

'He's been dead for twenty years, Peter.'

With the group fully assembled, the nighttime operation could commence. The first task was breaking in.

The former museum director had thought very carefully about how they should go about this, and most importantly why.

'It's almost like a mathematical equation,' she had told them, before embarking on an unnecessarily long and elaborate explanation.

She suspected the government had originally chosen option one. That option would then have been subjected to a confidential stress test, to forestall potential setbacks and cost increases further down the line.

But if they had now, just as confidentially, changed their mind at short notice, they couldn't possibly have had time for another stress test. And that meant no soil samples would have been taken along the planned route for option two, to check for coal tar oil or other pollutants from the past, which might necessitate a complicated clean-up. A surprise last-minute discovery on that route would therefore not be so surprising as to seem unbelievable.

When – that afternoon – Mrs Johansson had reached this point in her story, Julia was already halfway out of the door to track down a barrel of coal tar oil. But, with a deft sweep of her walking frame, the old lady managed to stop the mayor in her tracks.

'We don't want to poison the environment, Julia! Sit back down and let me finish.'

The mayor reluctantly complied.

Now, Halstaholm was special: hardly anywhere else in Sweden – apart from Gotland – had so many treasures been dug up over the centuries from the Stone Age, Bronze Age and Iron Age. Hence the important archaeological museum. People got particularly excited by the dwelling places, silver treasures and burial sites.

But eventually so many shields, Viking helmets and silver coins of exactly the same style had been donated to Halstaholm's museum that it was bursting at the seams. And the museum director took to storing the excess items in the attic.

At which point history took its course. Halstadäck went bust, Mrs Johansson retired, and Torsten the mayor closed the museum and sold the building to the would-be cook, who opened a pizzeria. The museum exhibits were sent off to Stockholm.

Except for the ones in the attic!

'I'm pretty sure they're still there,' said Mrs Johansson. 'And I've already made some discreet enquiries: my old key should open the pizza-maker's front door, no problem.'

Finally, Julia understood.

'You're a genius, Mrs Johansson! But did we really need the digression about coal tar?'

The former museum director explained with a smile that she had wanted to delay the big reveal for as long as possible.

And so it was that the taskforce was now standing in the dark outside the pizzeria, about to commit a break-in that no one would even notice. Quickly through the door, even more quickly up to the attic, fill a jute sack with historical artefacts, back outside, and lock up behind them. The next day, the pizza chef wouldn't be missing so much as a single mushroom or a basil leaf. In short, he would never know what had happened to him. As far as this had any bearing on him at all.

Everything went like clockwork. Carrying their booty, they set off in an easterly direction, heading for the precise coordinates Julia had googled earlier. With the help of Peter the Small's torch and the spade that the mayor had brought, they buried the treasure in a spot where it would most certainly not remain undiscovered until someone wanted to lay train tracks right there. They left the horns of a Viking helmet sticking out of the ground and scattered a few silver coins on the clay soil. Lastly, Julia brushed all their footprints neatly away, before taking a wild boar's trotter from her coat pocket.

'Where on earth did you get that?' Bosse Boules asked, impressed.

'I'm a woman of many talents,' said Julia with a smile, not admitting that her ex-boyfriend's mates had given it to him when they got engaged. They'd said that the foot should remind him to stop behaving like a pig – the worst kind of laddish humour. And it hadn't even worked.

Now the foot had come into its own. Julia made clearly visible tracks with it in the muddy ground. All the while with headlines in the back of her mind:

WILD BOAR DIGS UP SENSATIONAL VIKING HOARD IN SÖRMLAND

The secret nocturnal operation was over by two o'clock. Half an hour later, the group arrived back in Halstaholm. Mrs Johansson shuffled off home. Peter the Small climbed back up the ladder. Bosse Boules managed not to wake his wife. And soon they were all sleeping soundly in their own beds.

Only Julia sat, somewhat exhausted, on the sofa in her flat, having poured herself a glass of red wine and switched on the aquarium light.

'Were you asleep?' she asked the guppy. 'I just wanted to say, if we manage to pull this thing off, you're getting a name of your own. You'll be called Viking. Do you like it?'

Perhaps it was her exhausted state, or perhaps it really happened, but Julia had the impression that Viking nodded.

CHAPTER 20

The genius strikes again

Time to get down to business. Kenneth Carlander had a long list of definite and probable legal offences for which Julia Bäck was responsible. But since Hannes Marklund at the economic affairs ministry had given him to understand that he'd managed to turn option one into option two, the consultant would not have to make use of the charge sheet.

In Kenneth Carlander's mind, there was now no doubt that he was a genius. The finale of his Halstaholm trip had been particularly funny. He and the useful idiot Eriksson had gone to see Headteacher Gunilla Whatshername and put the thumbscrews on her. Figuratively speaking. Physical violence was for people who couldn't wage war with their brains.

Posing as a lawyer, he'd asked tricky questions about school attendance, and about who had instructed whole year groups to be released from vital parts of their education in order to play or cheer on a football match.

After the first few stammering and evasive answers, all lines of enquiry had ultimately led back to – you guessed it – Julia Bäck.

The consultant had to admit, despite her amateurish errors, this mayor had impressed him a little bit. Her charm offensive had nearly brought him down. Only his own outstanding intellect had saved the day!

Now that his three-million-krona consultancy fee was practically secured, he decided to splash a bit of that cash on making the finale as spectacular as possible.

He got hold of the errand boy he occasionally used for more straightforward tasks, and instructed him to decorate the outside of the factory in Frihamnen in black, red and gold fabric, lay on some German bratwurst for Kaltenbacher and his cockroaches when they arrived, and, at a suitable moment, unveil a statue or a bust of Franz Beckenbauer. And when the bloody German was beside himself with delight, he and Ingela Franzén could sit down at Carlander's desk, brought there for the purpose, and sign the contract with him.

Alas, Carlander was surrounded by idiots – though of course he'd known this already. The underling called back to say he couldn't find a statue of Franz Beckenbauer.

'There must be a bust or something, surely?' said Kenneth Carlander. 'How hard can it be? For God's sake, he played for Germany a hundred times!'

'A hundred and three,' said the imbecile. 'But it doesn't look like they made a statue or a bust of him for all his internationals. There's nothing you can buy anyway.'

'Then find some other bloody German!'

'Like who?'

'For Christ's sake, it doesn't matter who, as long as he's famous! Anyone except Günter Grass. Anything else, before I hang up on you? I've got my hands full achieving earth-shattering things here, and you're bothering me with trifles!'

No, there was nothing else. Although, the fool was just wondering if there were any special instructions for serving the bratwurst when the German and Mrs Franzén arrived.

'What are you *asking*? Do you need me to tell you how strong the mustard should be?'

'No, I just thought … we did something similar last year, for the party on the yacht. Shall I—'

This was too much for Carlander. 'Look, I'm busy solving all the financial problems of Sweden's capital city for the next twenty or fifty years – stop trying to draw me into a conversation about mustard!'

'Well, it's just that you—'

That was as far as the errand boy got; Carlander had hung up. And so history took its course.

* * *

Herr Dr Kaltenbacher and his daughters stayed at the Grand Hôtel as usual, just two blocks from Ingela Franzén's four-bedroom apartment on Östermalm. The German bed man had therefore kindly offered to give her a lift to Frihamnen. That meant they could also chat in the car. And so they arrived at around the same time as a text message from Kenneth Carlander saying that, due to one unfortunate mishap after another, he was going to be late.

The first thing Kaltenbacher, Franzén and the girls saw when they reached their destination was a factory façade completely covered in black, red and gold.

'How lovely!' Konrad Kaltenbacher said, honestly. But when they got out of the car, a silicone-enhanced bathing beauty came tripping over to them carrying an usherette tray of sausages. Just as Carlander's underling had instructed her, she purred in English, 'Now who would like a bratwurst, and maybe a little kiss to go with it?'

At the last summer party on the yacht, the sausages had been a runaway success. But, hovering in the background, the errand boy saw to his surprise that the giant-breasted sausage girl was not such a hit this time. Quick as a flash, he pulled the cord to unveil the bust he'd placed strategically beside the main entrance to the building. In the absence of Franz Beckenbauer, and having been expressly forbidden to use Günter Grass (whoever that was), he had chosen:

Karl Marx.

Herr Dr Kaltenbacher remained silent, but Ingela Franzén gave the errand boy a piece of her mind, asking him if he knew where the hell Kenneth Carlander was, and if he happened to have a loaded pistol he could lend her.

The next thing to happen was a nationwide beeping of mobile phones, with a push notification about a sensational archaeological find out east in Sörmland: coins and helmets, rooted up by wild boar, a find that turned on its head all previous research regarding the spread of the Vikings in both space and time. The head of the national Middle Ages collection had already made a statement. Given the government press conference that was due to take place shortly, he was asked about the new train line, which might now run right over this archaeological site.

To which the expert replied that in these latitudes, antiquity and modernity mustn't get in each other's way. It wasn't the first time there had been such a conflict of interest, and the find needn't impact the government's potential plans for the land. Though it would inevitably delay things. According to the head of the Middle Ages collection, a dig could begin as early as the following spring with absolute certainty, and be finished in twelve to twenty-four months. If no more unexpected finds came to light, that is. The museum director couldn't imagine that the train line – should the government opt for that route – would be delayed by more than three years.

* * *

Twelve minutes before the press conference on the government's rail strategy for the next fifty to a hundred years was due to start, the angriest economic affairs minister of all time entered Hannes Marklund's office.

Ayeh Mehdizadeh ordered her permanent secretary to sit back down as soon as he started to get up.

'Three years!' she cried. 'Do you have any idea how many elections can take place in three years?'

'One?' the permanent secretary ventured.

'Shut it!' Ayeh Mehdizadeh snapped. 'In twelve minutes' time we've got to present the government's carefully thought-through decision.'

'Probably more like eleven minutes now,' said Hannes Marklund.

'Didn't I just tell you to keep your mouth shut? You have exactly eleven minutes to dust off option one, so I can announce its implementation to the assembled press and claim it was our first choice all along.'

Hannes Marklund was lost for words. This had all happened so suddenly.

'But a Viking helmet or two—' he began.

'The press conference starts in ten minutes!' said Ayeh Mehdizadeh. 'Am I going to have a presentation script for option one ready by then, or will you be on your way to the airport to report for service as third secretary to the ambassador in Kyrgyzstan?'

'Do we have an embassy there?'

'If necessary, we'll open one.'

* * *

Nine and a half minutes before the live broadcast of the press conference, Julia's doorbell rang. The time was approaching eleven o'clock in the morning, but after a nervous wait the

Viking hoard had been discovered in the early dawn, and since then all hell had broken loose.

At the end of a long day, Julia usually liked to pour herself a little glass of wine, but this time she had filled a glass to the brim, and it wasn't even 11 a.m. Either there would soon be a reason to celebrate, or she would need to drown her sorrows.

Then the doorbell rang. She went to answer it.

'Magnus?'

'Hello, love. I happened to be in the neighbourhood, and—'

Julia shot him a dark look. 'No one ever just happens to be in Halstaholm if they can help it. Unless they have some specific reason. What do you want?'

Her ex-boyfriend grinned nervously. 'To be honest, I mainly came to see how Vincent is.'

'Who's Vincent?'

'The fish! Surely you haven't—'

'His name's Vincent?' said Julia. 'I've just told him he's called Viking.'

'Don't you remember? You know, when I came home that day and made that little confession ... that's when you got Vincent.'

'The fact must have escaped me,' said Julia. 'That he had a name, I mean. As I recall, there was quite a lot else to take in.'

Magnus smiled sheepishly.

'Yes, I know ... please forgive me ... it happened before I ... can't we—'

Julia Bäck slammed the door in his face. There were just three minutes to go until the press conference.

'But, Julia ...' she heard from the other side of the door.

'You just keep standing there, Magnus, and maybe in an hour or two I'll open up again. I've just got to go to the loo first.'

She sat back down on the sofa, decided to take a good swig of red wine no matter how the press conference turned out, and said to the fish: 'Vincent? What sort of a name is that? You're Viking, am I right?'

Kenneth Carlander was devastated at having arrived half an hour late. He hadn't meant to but she'd just been so *cute*, and over the previous evening and the night that followed, one thing had led to another. But what was important were the German colours on the outside of the factory, the bratwurst boy, the Franz Beckenbauer bust (or whoever it turned out to be), the press conference, the signed contract, the champagne toast – and the three million in Kenneth's account as thanks for his help.

He came to a screeching halt outside the factory in his gold Porsche. The German's black Audi was nowhere to be seen. Wasn't he here yet? Surely he couldn't have left already?

Instead, a skimpily dressed sausage-seller was standing there in a bikini, shivering and sobbing. And behind her – oh shit, who had put Karl Marx on a pedestal?

Kenneth looked around for the errand boy, who had one or two questions to answer. But in his place, he caught sight of the lead member for finance coming out of the factory doors.

'Morning, Ingela!' he said, though his voice was a little uncertain. Something wasn't right here.

'Kenneth!' said Ingela Franzén. 'How nice of you to drop by. Do come a bit closer so I can strangle you.'

CHAPTER 21

Dinner for two

'I was never worried,' Julia claimed when Konrad phoned.

'I was,' the German replied with a laugh.

'Julia!' the children shouted from the back seat. 'We're on our way to see you!' Then they started chanting, 'Hal-sta-holm! Hal-sta-holm!'

Konrad signalled to the twins to be quiet.

'But first, the three of us are going to celebrate at Gröna Lund. As I recall, you once said Halstaholm has everything except a swimming pool. If you'll permit me, I'll add an amusement park to that list.'

The plucky mayor just managed to stop herself recommending the car-tyre climbing frame in Halstaholm's park as an alternative. She promised to book a family room for Konrad and the girls at Hotel Halsta.

'And maybe afterwards, we can have something to eat at a nice restaurant while we sign the contract, what do you reckon?'

Konrad thought that sounded top-notch. About eight? The girls would be allowed McDonald's on the drive there, and then they would be fine on their own in the hotel room.

Having hung up, it occurred to Julia that there was a third thing Halstaholm lacked, besides a pool and an amusement park: a *nice restaurant* for dinner. She was reluctant to eat at the pizzeria she had broken into two nights ago.

'Bolmgren will have to solve the problem,' she told herself.

* * *

Kenneth Carlander was not accustomed to losing. When the member for finance had finished shouting at him because everything had gone tits up, he climbed into his Porsche, put his foot to the floor and drove back out to country-bumpkin territory.

'It ain't over till the fat lady sings, Julia Bäck,' he muttered to himself.

CHAPTER 22

Badehaus Beerhall

Bolmgren actually was a master chef! He had set up a table for two with a white cloth and candles beside the empty pool. The ladies' changing room had been partly transformed into a kitchen, while the men's was now the chef's private accommodation: bed, bedside table, reading lamp, desk and chair from IKEA. And a somewhat excessive bathroom with eight showers and as many sinks.

Julia arrived in time to check over the menu and all the details.

'You'll be having Maultaschen to start,' said Bolmgren. 'But we need to talk, Julia. Something has happened.'

The mayor was more focused on the here and now.

'Maultaschen? What's that?'

'Pasta filled with spinach, onions and my secret blend of herbs, sort of thing. But when can we talk?'

'And the main course?'

'Schnitzel, obviously!'

'Did you get hold of the beer I asked for?'

'I had to order it from Södertälje, but yes. When can—'

They heard a distant knocking from the pool's main door.

'He's here!' said Julia. 'I'll go and let him in – can you find a little side table for us? I need somewhere to put the contract.'

'Do you think my bedside table would be all right?' asked Bolmgren.

But Julia was already on her way down the stairs.

* * *

A few hours earlier, Kenneth Carlander and his useful idiot Hasse Eriksson had put their heads together.

First, they had marched straight through the unlocked door into the swimming pool, up the stairs and into the men's changing room. 'Use of a commercial premises for residential purposes!' Hasse Eriksson announced with great delight. But that wasn't interesting enough for Kenneth Carlander. For one thing, it was Bolmgren living here, not the mayor. For another, a tiny scandal like that wasn't going to make the German pull out.

Things got more interesting when the management consultant started opening the drawers in Bolmgren's rather forlorn desk. They contained a signed sales contract! No, two signed contracts!

'The council bought Bolmgren's house just before it blew up,' said Kenneth Carlander.

'Huh?' went Hasse Eriksson.

'And then Bolmgren bought the swimming pool.'

'Huh?' went Hasse Eriksson again. 'No, he's just renting it, isn't he?'

At that moment, Bolmgren came in. He had been preparing dinner in his makeshift kitchen when he heard noises coming from the men's changing room next door.

'What's going on?' he asked, recognising the troublemaker at once. 'Hasse Eriksson?'

Then he turned to Kenneth Carlander. 'And who are you, and what are you doing with my personal papers?'

Hasse Eriksson tried to think on his feet – not one of his great strengths. They had just been caught in the middle of something that very closely resembled a break-in.

'This is my lawyer,' was the first thing he could think of.

'Mr Kenneth ...' at which point Hasse realised it might be better not to give away his companion's real name.

Having a similar thought, the consultant came to his rescue: '... van den Obvious. Kenneth van den Obvious.' It might not be the best name, but he'd said it now. And under the circumstances, attack was definitely the best form of defence. Unfortunately, the sale agreement said nothing about an intention to blow up Bolmgren's house. But it was still a good starting point for Kenneth's plan.

'We've just come from the ruins of your house, Mr Bolmgren.'

'Oh, right, have you?' the chef said uncertainly.

His nervousness spurred the management consultant on.

'The investigation of the crime scene revealed that you owned an electric cooker, isn't that right?'

Bolmgren grew more nervous still. 'Yes – I mean, I don't entirely—'

'Not a gas cooker, then? Can you explain to me how a gas cooker that doesn't exist can blow up a house?'

'I'd been meaning to get one ...' Bolmgren went on, feebly, before realising that the answer wasn't going to help him.

Van den Obvious the lawyer waved the contracts in the air. 'We're taking these away as evidence,' he said, so firmly that Bolmgren didn't object. Carlander took advantage of Bolmgren's confusion.

'Don't go anywhere – we'll be right back,' he continued, and stalked back out to the Porsche, dragging Hasse Eriksson behind him.

Hasse tried to grasp what the management consultant was telling him.

'Why didn't you ask him about fertiliser or sticks of dynamite?' he urged.

'Because he would just have started asking for a real lawyer, and I didn't want to have to give these back!' said Kenneth Carlander, holding up the two contracts.

Hasse nodded. Carlander started the engine and pulled away.

'Where are we going now? To the police?'

'Not yet,' said the consultant. 'Where do you buy chicken feed and whatever in this miserable place?'

'That'll be Granngården; they sell agricultural supplies. But why go there?'

'A shop that sells chicken feed also sells fertiliser,' said Carlander. 'Now stop thinking, Eriksson, and just direct me there.'

One good thing about Halstaholm was that nowhere was very far away. They arrived less than five minutes later. Carlander parked the Porsche right outside the main door, where there wasn't a parking space, and peeled himself out of the car.

'Come on,' he told Hasse Eriksson. 'If you have to,' he added. 'But keep your mouth shut and let me do the talking.'

The shop was deserted. One lonely, bored woman stood at the checkout. Carlander made a beeline for her, with Eriksson in his wake.

'Hello,' he said. 'I'm a lawyer; van den Obvious is my name. Sorry for disturbing you like this in the middle of the lunchtime rush. If I say chemical fertiliser to you, what springs to mind?'

The cashier didn't look like she understood the question. Then she spotted the man standing behind the lawyer. 'Oh, hey, Hasse!' she said. 'Remember me? Camy, from school?'

Hasse Eriksson, who had been told in no uncertain terms to keep quiet, said nothing.

'For heaven's sake, answer the lady,' van den Obvious instructed.

'Oh, right, sure, I just thought … Hello, Camy, of course I recognise you. You've just got a few more wrinkles than you had back then … So, if I say chemical fertiliser, too, what springs to mind?'

Camy didn't appreciate being told that she wasn't as young as she used to be.

'What do you want me to say? Nitrogen, phosphorus, potassium and probably magnesium.'

'Who has bought that kind of thing recently?' asked the lawyer.

The cashier pricked up her ears.

'We're doing a crime-scene investigation,' Hasse explained.

Kenneth Carlander shot him an angry look that said now, in fact, he did need to keep his trap shut.

'Who's bought that kind of thing?' said Camy. 'Well, we have a range of organic fertilisers we recommend instead; we do live in the age of climate change, you know.'

Then she noticed the gold Porsche parked right outside the door.

'Are you planning to put the sacks of fertiliser in your car?'

The very idea made the consultant and pseudo-lawyer shudder.

'Why is it so bloody difficult to get a simple answer to a simple question in this town? Let me put it another way: how much chemical fertiliser did the mayor, Julia Bäck, buy here last week?'

Julia hadn't bought anything; it was a middle-aged man who paid for the stuff and lugged it out to the car park. Had she called him Bosse? But the mayor had been there – she'd loaded the purchases into her Volvo.

Camy didn't really want to tell them any of that.

'Who buys or doesn't buy NPK fertilisers from me doesn't concern anyone but the business and its customers.'

'Twenty bags?' asked Carlander.

'Good grief, no!' said Camy. 'Ten, at most.'

That was all Kenneth Carlander needed to know. He ordered Hasse Eriksson to 'Come!' like he was a dog, and walked out.

Hasse smiled uncertainly at Camy. 'Sorry about the wrinkles thing,' he said. 'You're actually still pretty presentable. Do you fancy—'

'Come!' yelled Carlander from outside.

* * *

In the swimming pool foyer, Konrad wrapped his arms around Julia and admired her beautiful red dress. Julia complimented his tie in return.

She led him up the stairs to the table set out on the poolside.

'How lovely!' said Konrad with a laugh.

'I'm sure Bolmgren has plans to cover the pool somehow, but I don't know the details. We can ask him when he gets here. Tonight he's chef, head waiter and barman in one.'

At which point Bolmgren appeared carrying a wine cooler filled with bottles of beer. He greeted his customers politely – the other matter would have to wait, he thought.

'I highly recommend this as an aperitif,' he said, showing them a bottle of Düsseldorfer Altbier.

Konrad Kaltenbacher burst out laughing.

'My dear Julia, how did you know …?' Then it occurred to him: 'The girls tipped you off, didn't they?'

Not at all. In fact, it had been his secretary, Frau Müller. She and Julia had had a few things to discuss, since the mayor needed more detailed information to have the factory contract drawn up.

'She's a lovely woman, Sabine, when you get to know her. She was a bit cautious to begin with, after the misunderstanding on the phone when we first spoke. But since then, she's warmed up.'

'You mean when you introduced yourself as "Julia Bäck" and she thought you said "Antony Blinken"?' Konrad asked with a smile.

Bolmgren withdrew, saying he'd be right back with the starter. Julia laid a hand on the stack of papers on Bolmgren's bedside table and said she had already signed the contract.

'Shall we start with your signature, or save it for dessert?' She smiled at him.

'Candlelight and pleasure first, and then work,' Konrad let slip, and then sheepishly backtracked. 'Oh, forgive me, Julia, that was going too far! It's just ... well, I feel so *relaxed* in your company. I let myself get carried away.'

Julia had to interrupt Konrad's stammered excuse. She said he hadn't gone too far at all, and could actually go a bit further if he felt like it.

'Why don't we talk about Paris while we're at it?'

That was the last but one thing she would say to Konrad Kaltenbacher for quite some time.

CHAPTER 23

Arrest warrant by candlelight

Naturally, Kenneth Carlander had planned everything and put those plans into action himself. But for this last part, he had to hand over to the useful idiot. He couldn't show his face in the scene that was about to take place.

The charges were a breach of the education act, and gross negligence or gross misuse of office – he would leave the legal niceties to the police. They needed to be given something to do, after all. Perhaps some kind of embezzlement charge could be worked out as well, because where had Bolmgren got the funds to start remodelling the swimming pool?

But the most important thing was: there was solid evidence of arson. Julia Bäck would be convicted of the crime in a heartbeat, if the police could just coax a couple of witness statements out of Bolmgren and wrinkly Camy at Granngården.

'Although, she wasn't actually that wrinkly,' said Hasse Eriksson.

'I don't care!' Carlander barked. 'Now go to the police, and get a move on! Here are the contracts ... and here are my notes in bulletpoint form. Just say nothing about my involvement, got that?'

'Kenneth Carlander, or Kenneth van den Obvious?' asked Hasse Eriksson.

'Both, you moron.'

* * *

Inspector Göran Klang was Julia Bäck's neighbour, and he was far from pleased about what was suddenly being demanded of him. Then again, these were serious allegations. The state prosecutor was on his way from Södertälje, Klang wrote out an arrest warrant for Julia Bäck, and the prosecutor said it looked like she should be taken into custody.

Hasse Eriksson had seen the table for two in the future beerhall and suspected Julia Bäck of planning a candlelit dinner with this German. He gladly tipped off the police about it before parking up his Mitsubishi outside and waiting for the suspect to be apprehended. When the inspector finally arrived in his police car, Eriksson leaped out and hastily offered to show him the way.

Which was how Hasse Eriksson came to be racing up the stairs into the swimming pool where Julia and Konrad were sitting, about to start discussing their Paris travel plans.

'There you are, you wicked criminal!' he shouted in Swedish.

Konrad didn't understand a word, but he could see that something had gone awry. All the more so when a uniformed police inspector appeared in the yapping man's wake.

'Calm down, now, Eriksson,' said Göran Klang. 'I'll take it from here.'

He turned to Julia. It was his sad duty, he said, to have to inform her that she was under arrest. He asked her to get to her feet and come with him.

'Handcuffs, just to be on the safe side?' Hasse suggested. 'Isn't she a flight risk? That man at the table with her is a foreigner.'

'Shut up!' said Inspector Klang.

'Julia, what's going on?' Konrad Kaltenbacher asked in English.

They had been *so* close. To saving Halstaholm, and to … well, there was something about Konrad that always brought a smile to her face when she thought about him, too. *So* close – and now, the exact opposite.

'I'll tell you what's going on: reality has caught up with me,' said the mayor in a resigned voice. 'Take care, Konrad, give my love to the girls … and please forgive me for everything.'

And she let the policeman take her away, with a combative councillor jumping for joy hard on their heels. Leaving Konrad Kaltenbacher sitting alone at the table.

Chef Bolmgren appeared from the ladies' changing rooms with the starter.

'Maultaschen,' he said. 'But where's your companion gone?'

'I don't know,' said Konrad truthfully. 'I think reality just came and got her.'

CHAPTER 24

The whole truth – almost

The lead member for finance was still in a foul mood. Traumbett had slipped through her fingers, and that dreadful bloody bastard Kenneth Carlander had left her in an impossible position. She never wanted to set eyes on him again.

Then her office door was flung open. There was only one person who would enter like that.

'Morning, baby,' said Carlander, a paper cup of takeaway coffee in each hand. 'Here comes *the wizard*, with coffee and cinnamon buns. No whisky before lunchtime, that's the rule.'

Something about his demeanour gave Ingela Franzén fresh hope. If everything had really gone down the toilet, why would he be strolling in here like this? Surely no one was that suicidal?

'Nor afterwards, if it can be helped. And I'm still not your baby. But what is there to celebrate? You haven't contracted a terminal illness, have you?'

The management consultant put one of the coffee cups down in front of Ingela, fished a bag of cinnamon buns from his coat pocket and settled down opposite her.

'Don't you read the news?' he said. 'The mayor of Halstaholm has been arrested, on suspicion of just about everything you can think of.'

'Arrested?'

'Yes, poor woman! But if she manages to keep her head out of the arson noose, I'm sure she'll be out of prison again in the summer.'

'And why does that make you *the wizard*?' was Ingela Franzén's next question. 'Was it you who got her locked up?'

Kenneth Carlander smiled mysteriously. 'I choose not to answer that question. But let's drink to the possibility of Frihamnen winning, in spite of everything!'

The lead member for finance caught a whiff of coffee and stretched out an arm for the cup. After taking a sip, she said thoughtfully, 'When Kaltenbacher called to let me know what he'd decided, he mentioned the advantages of the building, the low price and the future rail connection, which you didn't manage to divert. How have things changed since then, exactly?'

'But of course I managed to divert the train line! I can't help it if they then discovered a whole tribe of Vikings there. And now I've put Julia Bäck behind bars. If the German has half a brain cell, he'll steer well clear of doing any more business with the underworld.'

So nothing had been resolved yet. But at least there were grounds for hope.

'If you're right this time, I promise to reconsider, and you might get your fee after all.'

Taskforce meeting in Julia Bäck's office. Without Julia. But Bosse Boules, Peter the Small and Mrs Johansson were all there. And so was a copy of the *Halsta Nytt*, lying on the table. The headline leaped out at them:

AN END TO THE TRAUMBETT DREAM?
JULIA BÄCK IN POLICE CUSTODY

'Is it okay with you if I do some swearing?' asked Peter the Small.

'You're only ten, so not really,' said Mrs Johansson. 'But I think today we might make an exception.'

Peter nodded his thanks, and said: 'Shit.'

Just then, Harriet came in. She was carrying a small aquarium with a solitary guppy in it. 'Julia sends her regards from the cells. She's doing well in the circumstances, as they say. But she needs a fish-sitter for this fellow. His name's Viking.'

'Put him on the windowsill for now, and then I guess we'll have to draw lots,' said Bosse Boules.

While Harriet was doing that, she told them they had a visitor: the German and his two daughters were waiting downstairs in reception.

'Kaltenbacher?' said Bosse. 'What are we supposed to say to him?'

'*Entschuldigung* wouldn't be a bad start,' said Mrs Johansson. 'Will you ask them to come up, Harriet?'

The receptionist nodded and went out. Mrs Johansson carried on: 'And then I suggest we tell the truth and nothing but the truth, from beginning to end. What do you think?'

Bosse Boules nodded. Peter the Small agreed but said: 'Do you think we could leave out the bit about the Viking treasure? My parents still don't know I snuck out that night.'

'Maja thinks I was at a planning meeting,' said Bosse.

They heard footsteps on the stairs; the Kaltenbachers would be there any second.

'The whole truth,' said Mrs Johansson. 'Minus the bit about the Viking treasure. Okay?'

CHAPTER 25

Vegetable soup with envelope

The custody cells at Halstaholm police station were not large. They were each furnished with a table fixed to the wall, a chair and a hard bed, on which Julia was now sitting in prison clothes, staring blankly into space.

There was a knock at the door, followed by a jangle of keys. A guard came in with a tray.

'Good evening, Madam Mayor,' he said. 'I've got your dinner.'

On the tray was a bowl of vegetable soup, a glass of cranberry juice, a soft roll – and a white envelope.

'Thank you, Sebastian,' she said.

The two of them had been in the same year at school.

'How are you doing?' Sebastian enquired.

'Thank you for asking. I'm sure a few years behind bars will do me good.'

'Oh, don't be silly. Halstaholm is a small place, Julia, you know that. And the walls have ears. You can forget the arson business. It's bound to be just a few months somewhere nice, for an unfortunate oversight that resulted in you selling a swimming pool that didn't belong to you. And maybe because you inadvertently released the whole middle school from lessons.'

'Thank you for the comforting words,' she said.

'And don't forget the envelope,' Sebastian added. 'No idea what's in it, could be from the tax office. Those letters always seem to arrive at the worst moment.'

He said goodbye and left. Julia heard him outside, apologising for the fact he had to lock her in.

The until recently very enterprising ex-mayor made a start on the soup, which wasn't at all bad. And took a bite of the roll, which was less fun. Then she had a mouthful of cranberry juice and felt she was finished. Her appetite was not what it used to be.

She picked up the envelope, went back to sit on the bed, and began tearing it open to take a look at what she suspected was a tax bill.

As she was pulling out the thick wad of paper, there was another rap on the door. It was Sebastian, back again with coffee.

'I totally forgot this,' he said.

But what was up with Julia? She looked completely different from a moment ago. And she was waving a sheaf of papers at him.

'Didn't you like the soup?'

'He signed, Sebastian! *He signed!*'

'Who? The state prosecutor?'

'No, Kaltenbacher! The wonderful Konrad! Bloody hell, Sebastian, *he signed*!'

CHAPTER 26

Visiting time

Eight months in a penal institution – however open – don't make an ideal beginning for young love. But Konrad Kaltenbacher knew what he felt, and when he saw Julia again after five long weeks, he told her.

The visiting room in the women's prison was furnished with four wooden chairs, a table and a vase of plastic flowers on the windowsill.

'You've made me laugh and smile again, Julia,' said Konrad.

'Is that chair comfortable enough for you?' she asked.

'Not in the slightest,' said Konrad, who couldn't help but smile again. 'But seriously, I'm declaring my love here, and you come back with a question about the chair under my backside.'

Until recently, absolutely everything had pointed to Traumbett choosing Halstaholm. And of course she liked spending time with Dr Kaltenbacher. Even more so once he became Konrad to her. They had even talked about seeing Paris in springtime together!

But that had been when everything was motoring along at top speed. Since then, Julia had not only skidded off course, but ended up in a ditch.

Now the Traumbett boss was sitting in the least romantic room imaginable, declaring his love to her! To Julia, who had not only lied to him from their very first phone call onwards but had kept at it quite doggedly ever since.

'I'm not a good person, though, Konrad,' she said, gloomily. 'What if I can't stop going too far to get my own way? How would things turn out then?'

Konrad nodded and said he could understand Julia's self-doubt. In fact, he and the girls had discussed the situation at length at Hotel Halsta that fateful evening, and back at their house in Hamburg.

'Maren once asked me what was in this whole business for you.'

'How did she mean that?'

'What advantage you personally hoped to gain from it.'

Julia was deeply alarmed. 'Oh my God, no! I wouldn't ... I would never ...'

She couldn't find the words. But Konrad could: 'Exactly. You *are* a good person, Julia. You're a few sandwiches short of a picnic, you're impetuous, you don't always think before you speak or act ... in short, you're just wonderful, and I love you just as much as, if not more than, I hate the chair I'm sitting on.'

Julia let Konrad's words sink in. Though possibly not all the way.

'What about Frihamnen?'

The German told her that the one had no bearing on the other. He had chosen the best option for Traumbett on purely professional grounds. Consultant Carlander had somehow got hold of Konrad's mobile number and called to lay out assorted 'evidence' of Julia's various offences to him. As if that would have any impact on his purely professional decision.

'What did you say to him?' asked Julia.

'I don't like to use foul language,' said Konrad.

'I'd noticed that about you,' she said. 'So, what did you say to him?'

'I told him to piss off.'

And what if Konrad was right, and she did not need to hate herself? What if, in spite of it all, she was worthy of love? Then she could presume to give love, as well. To the man sitting on the wooden chair opposite her, for instance.

'Unlike mine, your picnic has a full complement of sandwiches, Konrad. You aren't impetuous in the slightest, and you think before you speak. Who knows, maybe that means we're made for each other?'

She smiled shyly. He took her words as a promise of some kind of future together.

'When's the next visiting time?' he asked.

'Not until Friday, but I'll talk to Hedvig.'

'Hedvig?'

She's the governor here. Married to Gunnar, a former bookkeeper at Halstadäck.'

'I'm sure Traumbett will need someone like Gunnar,' said Konrad.

'Would you be kind enough to drop in again tomorrow? Gentlemen callers aren't really allowed, but …'

'… But you'll talk to Hedvig?'

CHAPTER 27

Six months and three weeks later

Julia folded her prison uniform into a tidy pile and smoothed down the civilian clothes she had just put on. Then she tucked the last of her things into her hand luggage.

The cell door opened. A woman appeared in the doorway.

'It's time, Julia. I'm afraid we have to say our goodbyes. I'm going to miss you!'

'How will I manage without you, Hedvig?' said Julia with a smile.

'Brilliantly, I expect,' Hedvig told her.

And so Julia found herself back out in the open air. The remote women's prison was completely surrounded by beautiful countryside. The sun was shining on this glorious early summer day; it was the perfect weather for reclaiming your freedom.

She walked slowly out to the road and went to wait at the bus stop. The only sound was the birds singing.

Until the bus arrived. It slowed and came to a halt in front of Julia. The driver pressed the button to open the doors.

But she shook her head with a smile.

'Are you not getting on?' the driver asked, surprised.

'Thanks, but no thanks,' said the former mayor.

The bus wheezed off again, but it hadn't gone more than a few hundred metres before Julia caught sight of the next vehicle approaching. A black Audi A9 with German number-plates.

It stopped exactly where the bus had. Two girls, who had just turned ten, hopped out of the car, rushed over to Julia and threw their arms around her.

Konrad followed. With a quiet smile, he moved the pair gently aside and kissed Julia on the lips before taking her hand and leading her to the car.

'Come on, darling, let's go home to Halstaholm.'

The End

JONAS JONASSON was a journalist for the *Expressen* newspaper for many years. He became a media consultant and later on set up a company producing sports and events for Swedish television. He sold his company and moved abroad to work on his first novel. Jonasson now lives on the Swedish island Gotland in the Baltic Sea.